Du

The
WISHING
Jar

The
WISHING
Jar

A Novel

Penelope J. Stokes

DOUBLEDAY LARGE PRINT HOME LIBRARY EDITION

W PUBLISHING GROUP™
A DIVISION OF THOMAS NELSON, INC.
WWW.THOMASNELSON.COM

This Large Print Edition, prepared especially for Doubleday Large Print Home Library, contains the complete, unabridged text of the original Publisher's Edition.

The Wishing Jar

© 2002 Penelope J. Stokes.

Published by W Publishing Group, a division of Thomas Nelson, Inc., P.O. Box 141000, Nashville, Tennessee 37214.

This novel is a work of fiction. Names, characters, places, and incidents are either the products of the author's imagination or are used fictitiously. Any resemblance to actual events, locales, organizations, or persons, living or dead, is entirely coincidental and beyond the intent of the author or the publisher.

All poetry in *The Wishing Jar* is the original work of the author and may not be used without permission.

ISBN 0-7394-3372-5

Printed in the United States of America

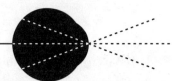

This Large Print Book carries the Seal of Approval of N.A.V.H.

5009

With special thanks to three people who have challenged me, encouraged me, and made my work a glory and a joy:

Ami McConnell,
Claudia Cross,
and
Judith Markham

Noble women all, and faithful friends

There are two tragedies in life.
One is to lose your heart's desire.
The other is to gain it.

—George Bernard Shaw

Prologue

The Very First Wish

Asheville, North Carolina
Spring 1904

The trail leading up Beaucatcher Mountain was rocky and steep, but the view from the top was worth the effort. Breathing hard from her exertion, Gracie Neal Quinn reached the crest and turned, gathered her skirts under her, and settled herself on the stone outcropping at the crest. Her thinking place. Her dreaming rock.

Long ago, in childhood, she had claimed this spot. From this vantage point, high above downtown, she had watched the city evolve and grow, even as she had transformed over the years from a wild, tomboyish girl into a cultured young lady, and now, at last, the cherished wife of Kensington Quinn.

Gracie lifted her head and took in the familiar vista. Down to the right, she could just make out Charlotte Street and the green-shingled roof and dark red brick of Quinn House, her new home. On the corner of Oak and Woodfin stood her alma mater, the Asheville Female College, and directly ahead the Vance Monument rose up in the center of Public Square, a great stone obelisk pointing toward the blue heavens. Opposite her on the far hillside, the rambling, ornate towers of the Battery Park Hotel loomed against the horizon. And beyond that, the misty, layered majesty of her beloved Blue Ridge, the mountains she had always called home.

When he heard her news, Kenzie would be furious with her for making the climb, but she had to get away for a while, had to think. Things had moved so rapidly in the past few months, and now another change. A change that would alter her life forever.

She pressed a hand to the small roundedness of her midsection. A baby, the doctor said. A child. A new life. A new little Quinn to carry on the name and the heritage of love she and Kenzie had begun.

Gracie closed her eyes and took in a

deep breath. Already she loved this child with all her heart and soul, and yet the responsibility of motherhood overwhelmed her. This wasn't just one baby. It was the future, stretching out before her like the mountains themselves, generation after generation.

She gazed once more at the hazy ridge beyond the Battery Park Hotel, where rich mantles of gray-blue and green and purple reached toward infinity, lifting their shoulders against a cloudless sky. "God," she murmured, "help me live up to my name. Let me bring grace and love to this child within me, and to all the generations that sleep in my womb."

For a long time Gracie Quinn sat on her thinking rock, letting her mind wander to thoughts of Kenzie and the child who would be born of their love. She imagined a fine strapping boy, strong and gentle like his father. Or perhaps an intelligent, adventurous little girl with her daddy's bright brown eyes and curious mind. They would come here, she and her children, and climb up this ridge to the place of dreams. She would share with them the wonder of the world, the glory of these mountains. Together they would watch the sun set and wish upon the first bright star.

Wishes.

What had the old peddler said about wishes?

Gracie reached into her bag, drew out a small wooden box, and opened it. Inside, cradled in a nest of dark green velvet, lay a ceramic ginger jar. She had bought it this morning on the street outside the market, only a few moments before she went into her physician's office. It was a small jar, no more than eight inches high, beautifully crafted, and very old. On both sides, bright against the smooth ivory porcelain, it bore the figure of a phoenix in flight, worked in red and gold.

Gracie had studied mythology in school and had become fascinated with the image of the phoenix. New life rising from the ashes. Singing as it died, and as it took flight once more. An ancient metaphor of new birth, of resurrection.

The peddler who had sold it to her had been a curious old woman, her bent body covered with a ragged, multicolored shawl. "It's a wishing jar," she had whispered, opening the box with a flourish. "Magic, you know. But only for the pure of heart." The woman had peered into Gracie's eyes. "Your heart is pure. Your soul is faithful. When the phoenix flies, your wishes will come true."

The peddler had quoted a price, and Gracie had handed over the money. She was not taken in by the claims of magic, of course. Still, the timing had seemed strange—providential even. She had come to town this very morning with a passionate wish in her heart, hoping the doctor would confirm what she suspected—that she carried new life within her . . .

She turned the jar over in her hands. The afternoon sun caught the gilding on the phoenix's wings, and for an instant it looked as if the bird were in motion, turning its head, gathering itself for flight. The scarlet plumage stirred, the golden feathers ruffled, and the bright black eye seemed to wink at her.

But it was merely a trick of the light. In the next moment, a wisp of cloud passed over the sun, and Gracie saw that the image was simply a beautifully painted bird on an antique ginger jar.

Laughing at her own foolishness, she replaced the jar in the box. Magic or no, it would be something she could hand down to her daughter—or her son's wife. Something the Quinn women could cherish for generations to come.

She got to her feet and started back down the mountain. It was time to go home and break the news to Kensington Quinn that he was about to become a father.

PART 1

What Might Have Been

*Every day of childhood
found me wishing for tomorrow
with all its glittering promise
and unseen possibilities.
Christmas, birthdays, weekends
at the beach
approached in slow motion,
but passed by in haste,
littering the sand with shattered toys
and broken shells.
I always thought
maturity brought wisdom in its wake,
yet still I lose touch with
this moment,
in reaching for the next.
Why does no one ever warn us
that tomorrow slips like water
through our fingers,
leaving us with only
thirst
and a misty memory?*

1

Nana's Legacy

Quinn House
August 2002

Abby Quinn McDougall stood transfixed, staring at the bookcase to the right of the fireplace. Five minutes ago, she had entered the living room on a wild tear, intent upon getting the dusting and vacuuming done as quickly and efficiently as possible. She had to be at work in an hour. Mama was in one of her moods this morning. Nothing Abby tried seemed to please her, so at last she had given up and turned to the cleaning that had been neglected for more than a week.

Housework, at least, didn't fight back. It surrendered easily to Abby's methodical, pragmatic touch and brought its own kind of pleasure—the satisfaction of seeing immediate results.

Abby liked results. Efficiency was her by-word, sometimes her obsession. And given the creeping chaos that could grow up overnight like kudzu, orderliness was not so much a personal preference as a matter of survival.

The dusting wasn't finished. The vacuum cleaner lay silent in the middle of the living room rug. Yet here she stood, unmoving, watching as a beam of sunlight, shot through with dust motes, spiraled down in front of her and landed as precisely as a well-aimed spotlight on a small white ginger jar decorated with a figure of a phoenix worked in red and gold.

The ginger jar, like this house, had been her grandmother Nana's, and Great-Grandma Gracie's before her, passed down through four generations of Quinn women. All of Abby's girlhood recollections included the memory of the jar, there in its place on the second shelf, displayed against the green velvet of its little wooden box. She passed the jar every day, dusted it every week.

Even as a child she had been mesmer-ized by the play of sunlight on the gold leaf, the curve of the phoenix's lush red tail feathers, the look in its eye as it tensed itself in anticipation of launching into flight. But sometimes, as now, a certain slant of light on the jar could send her thoughts back into the past, back to the days when she was a child without pressure or responsibility, back to those wonderful years when Nana was alive and everything seemed possible.

"This is a very special jar, child," Nana's whisper echoed in Abby's memory. "It's a Wishing Jar."

"A Wishing Jar?" Abby's child-voice, full of awe and hope, matched her grandmother's tone.

"Yes. Your great-grandmother—my mother—bought it more than fifty years ago, even before I was born. It's very old and very precious. Do you know what this is, this bird painted on the sides?"

Little Abby shook her head. "No."

"It's a phoenix, the great and powerful bird from mythology."

"What's missology?"

"Mythology," Nana corrected gently. "It's the tales people used to tell long ago. According to the story, the phoenix has the sweetest song in all the world. When its life is over, it goes up in flames and dies singing."

Abby felt the pain in her own heart and bit back tears. "That's so sad, Nana."

"But the story doesn't end there," Nana said. "When the phoenix dies, burned in its own nest, it rises up again, brand-new, out of the ashes of its old life. And then its song is sweeter than ever before."

"Like magic?" Little Abby had asked.

"Like a miracle," Nana had responded.

Even now, more than forty years later, with her grandmother dead for two decades, Abby could still feel that visceral response, the surge of wonder and childlike faith as she regarded the Wishing Jar and heard an echo of Nana's mysterious words: *"When the phoenix flies, your wishes will come true."*

Tentatively she reached out a finger and touched the phoenix, very lightly, on the feathers of its breast, then took the jar down from its place and held it in her hand. "If it could only be that simple again," she sighed.

What would her life be like, Abby wondered, if a drunk driver had not been on the road careening toward her husband that night? How much more simple would the world be for her if John Mac had lived? If Mama hadn't suffered the stroke? If—?

But *what ifs* were futile. Life wasn't simple, and never would be. Not for a widow in her fifties with an ailing mother and a difficult seventeen-year-old daughter. She could long all she wanted for a world without such stressful demands, but wishing wouldn't change anything. This was her life, with all its emotional bills and baggage.

And so she made no wish—not today, or for many years past. This ritual was merely a gesture to honor her grandmother's memory. Abby no longer believed in wishes, any more than she believed in prayer. She gave passing reverence to the Almighty, a nod of distant respect, but she no more trusted her petitions to be answered than she expected the Wishing Jar to grant her requests.

It was not always so. Once she had believed, both in the Wishing Jar and in the God to whom her grandmother prayed. She had been a little girl then, full of faith in magic and miracles and a loving, if shadowy, Deity. But even then her prayers had not been answered, nor had her wishes been granted.

Nana had tried to explain, but Abby's childlike mind could not comprehend. If the Wishing Jar really was magic, then whatever you wished should be fulfilled. If the Bible really did say, "Ask, and you shall receive; seek, and you shall find; knock, and the door shall be opened," then shouldn't it work for everybody, all the time?

Not according to her grandmother. It made a difference, Nana said, what you asked for, and why, and how. It mattered what kinds of desires and dreams and longings filled your heart.

"It's not like Aladdin's lamp, sweetie," Nana tried to explain when Abby complained about not getting her wish. "Some things are bigger than we can understand. The phoenix goes down into the flames singing, welcoming her fate. I wonder, does she know as she dies that she will rise up reborn? Or does she simply live to sing for as long as life will let her?"

Abby never forgot the question, even after Nana herself went down singing. But she never found the answer, either. Eventually she just let it go. Prayer, faith, the wonder of the Wishing Jar, Santa Claus, the Tooth Fairy—all of it put away like childish things that had no place in the efficient, orderly, rational life of an adult.

Yet something deep in Abby McDougall's heart still mourned the passing.

2

The Fiddler

Three hours later, Abby was still thinking about Nana and the Wishing Jar when a knock sounded on her office door. She looked up to see a tiny, well-dressed woman standing in the open doorway, striking a dramatic pose with her wild red hair thrown back and one arm leaning provocatively against the doorjamb.

"Birdie! What are you doing here?"

"Take the picture, quick! Here's your next cover shot."

Abby laughed. Carolyn Wren had been her best friend since childhood. In high school, Carolyn's petite stature and inexhaustible energy, coupled with her unusual last name, had earned her the nickname *Birdie*. It didn't matter that she was now the wife of Taylor Graham, the vice president of Western North Carolina University, or that she had built her own interior design business—she was still *Birdie* to all who knew her well. What she lacked in stature she made up in personality, and her effusive presence never failed to lighten Abby's mood.

Abby shuffled through the photographs scattered across her desk and held one up. "This is *Carolina Monthly,* not *Cosmopolitan,*" she said. "Unless you can transform yourself into a hummingbird or a waterfall or a late-blooming rhododendron, we're not interested."

"Kill-joy." Birdie abandoned her pose and came to sit on the edge of Abby's desk. "Working hard?"

"Hardly working. I can't seem to get focused today."

"Perfect. Come have lunch with me."

Abby gazed around the office, her eyes lingering on the proofs and photographs and blue-lined pages that occupied nearly every available horizontal surface. The offices of *Carolina Monthly* were on the top floor of the Flat Iron Building, and through the window between the filing cabinet and the bookcase, she could glimpse the Asheville skyline with rolling mountains behind and just a small wedge of an absolutely clear, deep, Carolina-blue sky. "Sounds tempting, but I have a deadline."

"You always have a deadline. And you always meet it, with time to spare. Come on. It's a beautiful day."

Abby threw up her hands in surrender. "All right. Let's go." She gathered up her bag and keys and stopped by her assistant's desk on the way out. "Ford, I'm going to lunch. If I get any calls while I'm out—" She held up her cell phone.

Birdie snatched the phone out of Abby's hand and placed it decisively atop an overflowing file on Ford's desk. "If she gets any calls while she's out, take a message."

Ford grinned, his round schoolboy face blushing in Birdie's direction. "Yes, ma'am— as you wish, ma'am." He gave her a snappy salute.

Abby looked from Ford to Birdie and suppressed a sigh. "I should be back by two. While I'm gone, could you sort through those photos on my desk and give me some recommendations for the piece on 'Biking the Parkway'?"

Ford nodded. "Be glad to. Anything else?"

"Just hold down the fort. See you later."

As they stepped through the front door of the Flat Iron Building into the September sunshine, Birdie linked her arm through Abby's. "I think Ford Hambrick's got a crush on me."

"He's fifteen years younger than you," Abby said. "Besides, half the men in Western North Carolina have a crush on you. And besides that, you're married."

Birdie's grin never wavered. "Of course I am, and very happily," she chuckled. "But you don't have to live on the mountain to enjoy the view."

⁓

They stood on the sidewalk outside Café on the Square, waiting for a table to open up. Across from them in Pack Square, a small crowd gathered to listen to a street musician. The Vance Monument rose like a lance toward the sky, and as the fiddler alternated between lively mountain tunes and plaintive ballads, the wavering reflection of the obelisk in the fountain below seemed to take on a life of its own, dancing and rippling in time with his bow.

Abby watched as the man lifted his bearded face to the blue sky and closed his eyes, immersed in the music. She went to the curb for a closer look. He wore faded jeans and a threadbare plaid shirt, but nothing seemed to matter to him except the late-summer sun on his face and the music that poured from his soul into his fiddle. For a brief moment, Abby was seized by a deep-seated longing, a nameless and unfathomable sadness.

Birdie nabbed a vacant table and called to her. Reluctantly, Abby dragged her attention away from the fiddler and sat down. The waiter appeared, and they ordered iced tea and grilled chicken salads.

"What would it be like, I wonder, to live with that much passion?" Abby murmured when the waiter was gone.

Birdie set down her iced tea glass and frowned. "What on earth are you talking about?"

"That musician. Look at him. He seems perfectly content and at peace. And it's obvious he loves what he's doing."

"He's playing for quarters on a street corner," Birdie said. "I don't see anything so fascinating about that." She narrowed her eyes. "You love what you're doing, too. Don't you?"

Abby forced her attention back to Birdie. "I guess so."

"You *guess so?* Abigail Quinn McDougall, you're the editor of one of the most respected magazines this side of the Continental Divide. You're a fabulous photographer and a successful writer. What else could you want?"

Abby shrugged. "I don't know. Just . . . *something.* For some time now, I've felt that something was missing in my life. I wish I knew what."

"What's missing is a relationship. I wanted to talk to you about that, in fact. Taylor has a new colleague, a professor in the Business School. I met him at the dean's cocktail party last week. He's good-looking, single—and straight. But he's new in town and doesn't know many people, so I thought maybe—"

Abby shook her head. "No. Absolutely not. I told you, Birdie. No blind dates. I'm not ready."

"When are you going to be ready, Abby? John Mac died more than two years ago. I know you miss him, but you've been shut up in that old house for far too long. Do you ever see *anyone* except your mother and

Neal Grace? And speaking of your mother, how is Edith?"

"Mommie Dearest?" Abby grimaced. "Sorry. I shouldn't have called her that. I love her, but she's a handful. Ever since the stroke she's been impossible, and getting worse all the time. The doctor says it's not unusual for a stroke victim to become depressed, or even hostile. She's lost so much—her independence, her dignity. Still, it's hard to take on a daily basis. I don't want to have to put her in a nursing home, but caring for her is stressful. As for my daughter—" She paused and sighed. "Neal Grace is—well, to be honest, I don't know how she is. Strange, mostly. Something's happened lately. She used to be so outgoing, so happy and well-adjusted. Now she keeps to herself a lot. And she seems—how do I explain this?—as if she's barely containing some kind of explosion."

"Do you think she might be experimenting with drugs? Sudden behavior changes can sometimes be a sign."

"I don't think so. We've talked about that in the past, and she's always been adamant about how stupid it is to do drugs. No, there's something else. I've tried to get her to talk about what's going on, but you know teenagers."

"Can't say that I do," Birdie answered, "having never known the joys of mother-hood myself."

Abby laughed. "If you want the experience, you can borrow mine anytime. At the moment I've had about all the joy I can stand." She shook her head ruefully. "I should have had children in my twenties, not my midthirties. At my age, I should be planning a wedding or bouncing a grand-child on my knee, not dealing with a rebel-lious seventeen-year-old."

"All the more reason you should get out a little. Now, about this new friend of Taylor's. His name is—"

Abby held up a hand. "Birdie, I'm fifty-one years old. I am not going to get involved with dating again. Especially with a younger man. End of conversation."

"Who said anything about being younger? He's fifty-three, married once, has two grown kids. And he's aging nicely, if I may say so." She laid a hand on Abby's arm. "Come to dinner next week. Meet him. No pressure. You never know what might happen."

"All right. Whatever."

"Do you mean it? How about next Thursday, at our house?"

"Sure, sure," Abby said, but she wasn't really listening. She was watching the fiddler again; he had seated himself on the edge of the fountain and was playing "Twinkle, Twinkle, Little Star" to a giggling baby in a stroller. His improvisation on the simple tune was entrancing—at least the baby seemed to think so.

Abby leaned down and rummaged in her bag.

"What are you doing?"

"Getting my camera. It just occurred to me, this guy would make a great story for the magazine. I'm going to ask him if I can take a few pictures, and try to set up an interview."

"Can you not stop working for one hour?" Birdie sighed, then waved her off. "Go on. I'll wait here and flag you down when our lunch arrives."

His name was Devin Connor, and he had the most incredible eyes Abby had ever seen. A clear, deep blue, like the cloudless sky over the mountains, like the watershed up on the Parkway, like the blue topaz ring she had inherited when Nana died. His face, weathered by sun and wind to the color of toffee, was seamed with craggy lines. His hands held the fiddle as if it were alive, an infant cradled against his chest.

Abby introduced herself and briefly explained what she wanted. He caught her gaze and held it for a moment, then brushed a lock of hair away from his forehead and nodded. "Yes," he said quietly, "yes, I suppose I would be willing to do that. There's little in life that pleases me more than talking about my music"—he paused and grinned—"unless, of course, it's *playing* my music."

She handed him her card. "My office is in the Flat Iron Building. Could you call or come by tomorrow?"

Nodding his agreement, Devin Connor took the card, stuck it in his back pocket, and resumed playing. Abby took a few photographs—the Vance Monument in the background, some closeups of his hands on the fiddle, a nice shot of him leaning down next to the laughing baby, and one of his reflection in the fountain. Then she waved good-bye and left, dropping a ten-dollar bill into the fiddle case when he wasn't looking.

3

Neal Grace

Neal slid her key into the lock and tried to open the front door quietly so her grandmother wouldn't pounce on her. Sometimes Granny Q reminded her of a cat waiting for a mouse to stick its head out of a hole. For someone who had suffered a stroke, she had surprisingly good hearing, and even better instincts. Neal couldn't often put anything over on her grandmother, but that didn't stop her from trying.

She felt a finger poking into her back. "Hurry up, will you?"

Neal grimaced. T. J. Sweet might be her best friend, but sometimes she could be the densest, most frustrating person on the face of the earth.

She turned and frowned at T. J. "Shhhh!"

"Why are you whispering?" T. J. asked in a voice about ten decibels above normal.

"Because I don't want to rouse the dragon," Neal hissed.

"Your grandmother, you mean? That sweet old lady? What's the big deal? You come home from school and bring your best friend with you. Not exactly a capital crime."

"I'm just sick of everybody knowing my business all the time, all right? Now, if you'll just be quiet, we might be able to sneak in and get upstairs before she knows we're home." Neal leaned on the door, and it gave a loud creak as it swung open. She groaned.

"That you, NeeGrace?" a garbled, wavering voice called from the kitchen.

T. J. grinned. "It's us, Granny Q!" She dropped her book bag on the sofa and grabbed Neal by the arm. "Come on."

Reluctantly, Neal followed her friend into the kitchen. Granny Q stood beside the stove with the oven door open. The acrid smell of something burning filled the air, and a thin haze of blue smoke hovered near the ceiling.

"T'resa? Little T'resa Joy Sweet!" Granny Q tried to smile, but her mouth was still paralyzed on the left side, so the expression came out more like a grimace. Her words slurred, and her left eye had the droopy, bloodshot look of a hound dog. "Come in, children. I made cookies—'cept I burned 'em jus' a little."

Neal dragged herself into the room and slouched into a chair at the kitchen table. She fixed her eyes on her hands, on the wooden tabletop—anywhere except her grandmother's face.

"They look just fine, Granny Q," T. J. was saying. "They're not real burned. We can just scrape off the bottoms, and—"

"I don't want any," Neal interrupted. "Let's go up to my room, T. J. We've got homework."

"Nonsense," her grandmother said, but the word came out as *nunshens.* "You girls need a snack after school. I baked 'em special." She shuffled over to the refrigerator, bracing herself against the counter, and took two glasses out of the cabinet. Neal watched out of the corner of her eye as her grandmother tried to pour milk, sloshing it onto the floor. She looked away and gritted her teeth.

"Here, let me help," T. J. said brightly. She took the half-gallon jug and finished pouring, then retrieved a paper towel from the roll and mopped up the mess.

Granny Q lurched over and sat down opposite Neal while T. J. set the milk and cookies on the table. "How was your day at school, NeeGrace?"

"Fine."

"Don't wan' some milk and cookies?" She pushed the plate in Neal's direction with a spotted, palsied hand.

"No."

Neal ducked her head, trying to avoid meeting her grandmother's gaze. But she couldn't help seeing the tear that leaked out of Granny Q's bad eye, matched by a string of saliva that crept from her sagging mouth. Anger boiled up in her—an acidic, unpredictable, unstoppable rage.

She didn't want to see this. Didn't want to be anywhere near her grandmother. Everything about the old woman disgusted her. The grotesque, twisted face. The way she sidled into a room, dragging her numb left side behind her like half a cadaver. The pale legs webbed like a road map with purple varicose veins. The flat, ugly feet sheathed in dirty chenille bedroom slippers.

And the smell. The smell was the worst of

all. It wasn't body odor, exactly, but a hot, stale, medicinal smell.

Neal vividly recalled the days when Granny Q smelled like lavender water and lilac powder, when she smiled without drooling and spoke complete sentences that could be understood without an interpreter. She remembered childhood Christmases in this house, with an enormous tree in the front foyer and lights everywhere, with Mom and Dad laughing, and Granny Q and Grandpa Sam handing out presents like Mr. and Mrs. Santa Claus. In those days the entire house filled up with delicious aromas—fresh pine and apple pies and turkey and homemade yeast rolls.

But that was before. Before Grandpa Sam's heart attack. Before her own father's death in a head-on collision with a drunk driver. Before the stroke that took Granny Q away and replaced her with this—this walking corpse.

Neal tried to push the memory of her father from her mind. She missed him so much that she didn't dare think about him. The pain of losing him was like a bottomless pit, a vacuum at the center of her soul—if she got too close, it would suck everything inside her into the darkness. She could almost imagine herself being pulled inside out and then vanishing completely.

No. She couldn't go there. Not now. Maybe not ever.

It was partly her fear of the vacuum that made her so eager to come and live at Quinn House with Granny Q. Here, at least, Daddy's memory didn't pervade all her senses. The sturdy old brick house, with its dark green roof and shaded porches, had been in the family since the early 1900s. Yellowed photographs of the Quinn ancestors lined the walls, and above the marble fireplace in the living room hung the family crest, emblazoned with the Quinn motto: *Purity of Heart, Faithfulness of Soul.*

By the time she was five, Neal had memorized the motto and knew all of her ancestors by name. She would walk slowly along the walls, pointing to the photographs and identifying each one. Kensington Quinn and his wife Gracie, the first of a long line her mother referred to as "the strong Quinn women." Then their daughter, the original Abigail, whom Mom called "Nana," with her husband, James Nelson. Photos of James and Nana's three children were there, too—

the sons who had died in the war and the surviving girl, Edith Quinn Nelson, a radiant bride on her wedding day.

Neal would never forget the first time her mind connected that dazzling young woman in the photograph with her beloved Granny Q. Her grandmother, all dressed in white, bright-eyed and shimmering, with a handsome, younger version of Grandpa Sam standing proudly at her side. She remembered climbing onto a small stepstool and putting her nose close to the glass, inspecting every detail of Granny Q's face, tracing the eyes and nose and mouth with one finger. This was the grandmother she adored. And she had once been fresh and beautiful, with smooth, bright skin and eyes that didn't crinkle at the corners.

All her life Neal had been awed by those photos and the heritage they represented. A legacy of character and love and family loyalty—five generations of it, counting Neal herself. Nearly a hundred years of Quinn history. She could close her eyes and see those faces. Sometimes at night when the house was quiet she imagined she could hear their voices, whispering to her on the breeze: *Pure of heart . . . of heart . . . of heart . . .*

In her younger days, before she knew better, the idea of that legacy brought her comfort, made her feel part of something special, something important. But after Daddy's death and Granny Q's stroke, everything changed.

No longer did Neal relish the idea of becoming "one of the strong Quinn women." She had seen, firsthand, how quickly strength could turn to weakness. Every time she looked at her grandmother, a caustic and troubling thought rose to the forefront of her mind: If this was the reward for being pure and faithful, she wanted no part of it.

Laughter drew her back to the present, and Neal looked up to see T. J. smiling, holding her grandmother's hand, talking animatedly, as if everything were perfectly normal. A weight pressed in upon her, and for a moment she couldn't breathe.

At last she found her voice. "I . . . I'm not feeling so good, T. J. I've got a headache. Think I'll go upstairs and lie down for a while. See you tomorrow."

Before T. J. or Granny Q could protest,

Neal jumped up from the kitchen table and fled the room.

She was halfway through the living room before she could catch her breath. Panic roared through her—the kind of blind terror that comes with total darkness, the fear of being buried alive, locked in a mausoleum with only the dead for company. These feelings had been coming on for months—years, maybe. Certainly since Granny Q's stroke six months ago, perhaps even since Daddy's death—or at least since moving into Quinn House. The sensation of being trapped, not able to breathe, not at home in her own skin.

Claustrophobia. Yes. That's exactly what it felt like. The walls—these stout brick walls mortared together with Quinn family character and loyalty—were closing in on her.

Neal sank down on the sofa and stared with unfocused eyes at the family crest over the fireplace. Behind her, in the kitchen, she could hear the muffled voices of T. J. and her grandmother. Talking about her, probably. Wondering what had gotten into her.

She couldn't help wondering the same thing.

All her life she had lived up to the expectations presented to her. She did well in school, never got into trouble, always made friends easily. Her mother trusted her, and the two of them got along pretty well. Why, then, did she feel so . . . so *suffocated?* Why did she want nothing but to get away, to be anywhere but here, where the heritage of her Quinn-ness pressed in upon her like stone walls of solitary confinement?

Even her name betrayed her: *Neal Grace Quinn McDougall,* after her great-great-grandmother, the matriarch of the clan. Every single woman in the family bore the Quinn name in one form or another. She could never get away from it, no matter how hard she tried.

A flash of light and movement caught her eye. A breeze had rustled the leaves outside the living room window, and shadows played across the bookcase next to the fireplace. Her eye was drawn to the old ginger jar that sat on the second shelf.

The Wishing Jar, Mom called it. Another piece of history, handed down through the generations. One more symbol of what it meant to be a Quinn.

Neal watched the interplay of light and shadow over the jar. It almost looked as if the phoenix were moving, ruffling its wings in preparation for flight.

She would fly away, too, if she could.

She leaned back against the sofa cushions and closed her eyes. "God," she murmured, "I wish my life were different."

4

Granny Q

Edith Quinn Long braced herself against the wall in the dimly lit hallway and stared up at the photograph of herself and her husband on their wedding day. She had been so young back then, just after the war, so innocent and full of expectations. Sam, bless him, had been a basket of nerves the whole week leading up to the wedding, and for a brief while Edith had wondered if he had gotten cold feet and wanted to change his mind.

"Land sakes, woman," he had blustered, "I never heard such a ridiculous idea in all my born days!" He had gentled then, seeing her fearful expression, and stroked her hand while he explained. "I've never done this before—getting married, I mean. And I never intend to do it again. You're the only woman who could ever fill up my heart. The vows I'll take—and gladly, mind you—go straight to the ears of God. That makes it a serious matter, between myself and the Almighty. And you, of course."

He had smiled into her eyes and kissed her. "Come Saturday, when the legalities are out of the way and my ring is on your finger, I won't be so all-fired wound up. We'll be happy, you wait and see. Our life together is all I've ever wanted, so don't go worrying yourself over nothing."

He had been right, Edith recalled. They *had* been happy—gloriously, deliriously happy. With Sam there had never been a moment when the honeymoon ended and dull routine set in. Always, they had taken delight in one another—and in little Abby, once she came along. Sam had been a wonderful father, and after Abby's marriage to John Mac and the arrival of Neal Grace, an even better grandfather.

Strange, Edith thought, how the past could wind around your heart and not let go. She could still see him, laughing by the fire as he wrestled on the floor with his granddaughter. Making a solemn ritual out of carving the Thanksgiving turkey. Padding his slim frame with bed pillows—pillows that saved him a broken bone or two that Christmas Eve he got the crazy notion to climb up on the roof so little Neal Grace could hear Santa arrive.

Sam had been dead nearly five years now—and yet he remained. In her heart. In this house. In the legacy of love he had left behind. She could hear echoes of his voice every time the wind blew through the eaves, and the scent of him—cherry pipe tobacco and Old Spice—permeated the walls like incense.

At night sometimes he called to her, floating through her dreams, caressing her skin on a breeze. She had never known, until Sam died, how thin the walls could be between this world and the next—so thin that at times she almost felt she could see eternity, like looking through a sheer curtain into forever.

She *had* peered through, just once, the night of her stroke. When the lightning bolt in her head had struck, turning her legs to jelly and leaving her lying helpless on the living room rug, she had felt Sam so near, touching her, holding her hand. The pain and fear had vanished, and through her closed eyelids she had seen him, beckoning to her, urging her forward.

At that moment, she had wanted nothing more than to follow him. She lay there, eagerly awaiting the end and the new beginning, praying with all the faith she could muster that no one would interfere until she had made it to where Sam waited on the other side.

But Abby found her. Sirens and flashing lights pierced the darkness. The agony in her head returned. Unfamiliar faces hovered over her like vultures, and when she tried to scream, to tell them to leave her alone and let her go, her voice failed her and she couldn't speak.

The doctors said it was a miracle she had lived and told her that, with dedication to a program of physical therapy, she might regain even greater use of her paralyzed arm and leg. But the therapy was painful and exhausting, and Edith had no heart for it. What was the point? She would still be here, wouldn't she, without the man she loved, without any reason to go on?

And so Edith dragged her numb left side through empty days and even emptier nights, listening to Sam's whisper under the eaves and forcing herself to get up every morning and pretend to be happy that she had cheated death.

She hadn't tried to explain her feelings to her daughter or her granddaughter or her friends. No one would understand. She was alive, after all, and didn't everybody say that life was precious, no matter what kind of life it turned out to be? Didn't she have her daughter and her granddaughter to console her and care for her in her waning years? She was, people kept telling her, one of the lucky ones.

Edith lurched on down to the end of the hall and paused to catch her breath, propping one hand on the small walnut chest that stood at the lower landing. The antique mirror hanging above it was cloudy and spotted with age, but she could still see her reflection. The woman who stared back at her was barely recognizable as the same one in the wedding photograph. One side of her face hung slack and loose, unable to respond to her brain's commands. Words came out of the distorted mouth slurred and unintelligible, even to her own ears.

But she could still see, could still hear. And she saw how Neal Grace looked at her, heard the unspoken revulsion between every muttered word that passed for conversation. The girl could barely stand to look at her. The magic between them was gone.

And it had been magic. For years there had been a bond connecting Edith's heart to her granddaughter's—stronger, if such a thing were possible, than the connection she had with her own child. Most children adored their grandparents, of course. They enjoyed being spoiled and pampered and doted on. Grandparents could love their grandchildren unconditionally, leaving the complications of discipline and training and correction up to the parents.

But with Edith and Neal Grace, it was more than that. Much more. Since the moment of that child's birth there had been a kind of soul-bridge between them, an understanding and commitment that went unspoken because it was far beyond the realm of any words. Minutes after her granddaughter's birth, Edith had held the squirming, squalling infant in her arms and breathed on her, watching in wonder as the baby settled down, closed her eyes, and nestled into her grandmother's arms as if she had found a second comforting womb.

Perhaps the bond had been forged because Abby had been so weak after the difficult delivery, and Edith had stepped in to care for the baby. Or perhaps Neal Grace simply sensed the love in her grandmother's touch and responded to it. Whatever the case, from the instant Neal Grace made her entrance into the world, she had been her grandmother's child.

Until now.

Now the girl kept to herself, hiding in her room behind a closed door, spending as little time as possible in the common areas of the house. She spoke only when it was absolutely necessary, and despite her mother's constant reprimands, didn't seem to care that she was being rude.

Edith tried to tell herself that Neal Grace was only going through a phase, being a rebellious teenager, and that she would grow out of it. But she knew better. The girl she loved so fiercely was . . .

Ashamed of her.

Edith looked up the stairs. She couldn't see her granddaughter's room from this vantage point, but she knew the door would be closed. It always was. Muffled music drifted down from overhead. She couldn't hear the words, and doubted she would have understood them had she been standing right next to the stereo speakers. For a moment she hesitated, longing to go upstairs and talk to the child, to try once more to reestablish the bond that somehow had been severed.

But it was no use. Slowly, painstakingly, she reversed course, limped into the living room, and sank down onto the sofa in front of the fireplace.

It was beginning to get dark. Abby would be home soon. They would have another stilted, awkward dinner, just the three of them, and then Neal Grace would retreat into her own world again.

Edith sighed and leaned back against the sofa pillows. Her eyes came to rest on the bookcase next to the fireplace, on the small ginger jar her own grandmother Gracie had bought from a street peddler nearly a hundred years ago. Outside, a car turned the corner in front of the house, and the headlights cast a faint sweep of bluish light in an arc across the wall. The gilding on the phoenix caught the light and sent it flashing, as if the bird had ruffled its wings.

"When the phoenix flies, your wishes will

come true," Edith murmured, recalling the long-held family legend.

And what would she wish for? That her life would turn out different? That she wouldn't be such a burden to her daughter, such an embarrassment to her grand-daughter?

It didn't matter what she wished. Wishing didn't make it so.

And yet her heart betrayed her, and she found herself wishing she could be with Sam again.

5

The Sky and the Stars
and the Music

All afternoon, as she worked with Ford putting the final touches on the October issue, Abby had not been able to rid her mind of the image of the fiddler Devin Connor with his eyes closed and his face turned toward the sky. The music swirled through her mind like wood smoke, permeating her senses with its haunting refrains.

"Abby, come back to earth," Ford said for the third time in an hour. "That photograph doesn't go there; it goes here." He leaned across her and clicked the mouse, dragging the photo across the screen. "It's nearly five. How about if we call it quits and finish this tomorrow?"

Relieved, Abby left Ford to tidy up the office and made a quick exit. She had intended to drive out to the Farmer's Market, pick up a few fresh vegetables for dinner, and make Mama a real meal rather than a collection of leftovers stir-fried in the wok.

But she didn't. Instead, she found herself heading in the opposite direction, northward up the Blue Ridge Parkway, past the watershed, past Craggy Gardens, all the way to Mount Mitchell.

It was nearly dusk by the time she pulled into a deserted overlook, dug in her bag for her cell phone, and punched in her home number. After four rings, the answering machine picked up. Her mother would hear it, even if she wouldn't answer the phone.

"Mama, it's Abby. I'm going to be a little late, but don't worry. I'll fix dinner when I get home. If Neal Grace shows up, tell her not to go anywhere tonight."

She hesitated for a second, then added, "Love you. Bye."

For a second or two she waited, watching until the green screen on the phone went to black. Then she got out and sat on the warm hood of the car, facing the mountains.

Below her, evening mist hung like stretched cotton in the layered valleys between the mountain ridges. The setting sun illuminated the clouds above the farthest range with a red-gold hue, and the sky deepened from blue to dusky purple to navy.

Abby could feel it in her body—a creeping lethargy, as if earth's gravity were gradually increasing and no one else had noticed. Every morning the weight seemed greater, the sheer effort of existence more demanding. Every night the yoke lay more heavily upon her, the burden of making a living, caring for Mama, trying in vain to keep Neal Grace connected to the family.

And remembering not to scream out loud where anyone could hear.

What had become of the life she had always envisioned when she was younger and the branches of the world hung low with ripe possibilities, waiting to drop fruit into her hand? Her heart answered before her mind had a chance to object. She knew what had happened. John Mac had died.

Abby had never subscribed to the unhealthy notion that marriage was "two halves seeking to form a whole." She had been whole when she met John McDougall, and no one on earth would have described him as half of anything. They hadn't *needed* each other to make life complete.

And yet, when they fell in love, something miraculous had happened. Abby had found herself opened to an entirely new dimension of light and depth and color and music, as if she had been living in black and white and suddenly turned the corner to find the world painted with a thousand brilliant hues. John Mac's love for her—and hers for him—changed everything.

She soon discovered he had a gift for changing lives. As director of Blue Ridge Enterprises, a small nonprofit organization, he helped the underprivileged develop sustainable businesses. He pointed with pride to the city's numerous restaurants, shops, and home-based endeavors now owned and operated by men and women who had once lived on welfare and fed their families with groceries from the shelves of local food banks.

Everyone who knew John McDougall loved him. When he and Abby married, their elaborate reception was catered, free of charge, by Christine, a single mom whom John Mac had helped turn her cooking and baking skills into a profitable business. They were chauffeured to the ceremony by Willie, who now owned a fleet of eight stretch limousines, thanks to John Mac's assistance in financing his first taxicab.

Abby had been so proud of him, so awed by his selfless giving. Every life he touched was transformed for the better, including hers. With John Mac, love was the norm and loneliness a distant memory.

Abby had never even considered that her residence in this bright new world might not be permanent, that someday she might have to return to the old black-and-white, two-dimensional life. Until a drunk driver in a speeding car ripped away the light and color and shrouded her world in shadow.

Now she was back in that gray, flat land, and she had no idea what to do next, where to go from here.

What kind of life could she build without the man she loved? How could she regain the light and the color and the music? Abby wasn't certain. She didn't know what she wanted—only that this wasn't it, this daily grind of deadlines and sameness and stress.

She ought to be grateful, she supposed. She had an interesting job, a beautiful old house that had been in her family for gener- ations, a healthy bank account, good friends. But no one else, not even those who knew her well, could understand how she felt inside. The gnawing in her gut, the tensing of every nerve, the black hole at the pit of her being that threatened to swallow her whole.

The final rays of sunlight faded from the high clouds. Abby turned her face up toward the darkening sky. Behind her closed eyelids, she could see the image of Devin Connor, playing his fiddle first to the heavens and then to the laughing child in the stroller. She could hear the childhood tune, its simple threads woven with passion and purpose into an intricate melody. *Twinkle, twinkle, little star . . .*

She opened her eyes. At the edge of the horizon, where the ebony hips of the mountains butted up against the sky, the first star winked on. Like a small, bright candle beckoning her forward.

Still Abby sat there, watching. As the darkness deepened, more stars appeared—thousands, millions of them, close enough to touch, yet a lifetime away. Galaxies upon galaxies, calling to her, whispering secrets on the humid night air.

Abigail Quinn could not understand the

voices of the stars. And yet for the first time since John Mac's death, she felt a tiny stirring within her, the weak but determined heartbeat of hope.

~

Abby's newfound sense of promise vanished the moment she stepped foot over the threshold of her own home. Mama sat unmoving on the sofa in the living room—in the dark. Abby could hear rock-and-roll music coming from upstairs. Obviously Neal Grace was home, sequestered in her room.

Stifling her annoyance, she made a sweep of the living room, snapping on lights, until her circuit brought her back around to her mother. "What are you doing sitting in the dark?" she said.

She hadn't intended it to come out as an accusation, and yet her tone betrayed her. As soon as she looked into Mama's eyes and saw the wrinkled, sagging face streaked with tears, she regretted her harshness. She sat down and took her mother's hand. "Mama, what's wrong?"

Her mother said nothing, just lifted one shoulder—the right one, the good one—in a shrug.

Abby closed her eyes and prayed for patience. Then her nostrils caught the lingering scent of something charred, and she jerked her head up. "Mama, did you use the stove today?"

Like a naughty child caught in an act of disobedience, Mama lowered her eyes. "Yeshh. Baked cookies for girls."

"You baked cookies for the girls?" Abby repeated. "What girls?"

"NeeGrace and T'rese."

"Teresa? You mean T. J.?"

Mama nodded. "But I burned 'em. And spilt the milk."

Abby shook her head. "Ah, Mama, what am I going to do with you? You know you shouldn't be trying to cook when I'm not here. You could hurt yourself."

"Sorry." Mama bit her lip.

"It's all right." Abby gave her mother a quick hug. "I just worry about you. Promise you won't do it again?"

When Mama nodded assent, Abby got to her feet, extended both hands, and forced her face into a smile. "Come on, then. You can keep me company while I fix supper."

Together they shuffled into the kitchen, Abby slowing her pace to match her mother's. When Mama was settled in one of the chairs next to the table, Abby turned her attention to the problem of dinner. She opened the freezer and peered in.

"We've got two family-sized entrees: one chicken pasta, one lasagna," she called over her shoulder. "Which one do you want?"

"Chicken," Mama said.

"OK, chicken it is. That's Neal Grace's favorite anyway." Abby retrieved the chicken pasta from the freezer and read the instructions to herself as she removed the shrink-wrap. *Preheat to 350.* She turned toward the stove and saw a little red light glowing next to the oven controls. Not only had Mama burned the cookies, she had forgotten to turn off the oven. "Step one," she muttered. "Looks like the preheating's done."

⌒

Edith saw the red light on the stove the minute she came into the kitchen. She had hoped Abby wouldn't notice, or that there might be a chance for her to cut the oven off when Abby's back was turned. No such luck.

She braced herself for another lecture, but apparently her daughter thought she had suffered enough for one day. Instead of commenting, Abby simply slid the foil pan into the oven and pulled a bag of romaine and a couple of ripe tomatoes out of the crisper in the bottom of the fridge. "Want to help me make salad?"

Edith nodded. Abby washed the vegetables, patted them dry with a paper towel, and set them, along with a big wooden bowl, on the table in front of her. Then, apparently reconsidering her initial salad strategy, she took the tomatoes back. "I'd better do the cutting," she said.

Abby, of course, wouldn't let her near a knife. Suppressing a sigh, Edith began tearing the lettuce into smaller pieces. Even this small task was a challenge, because her left hand didn't work so well anymore. She had to *think* about every move—how to grab each leaf between her left thumb and forefinger, hold it, and then tear pieces off with her right hand. It was a good thing the pasta would take forty minutes to bake. By then, she might have the lettuce finished.

Surviving a stroke had proved to be much more humiliating than being found dead on the living room carpet. In one terrible instant, Edith had become a child again, unable to tie her own shoes or cook a meal in her own kitchen. For weeks after she first left the hospital, she couldn't even go to the bathroom or take a shower alone. Why, she wondered, did a stroke have to split a body down the middle like that? She would have given up her good leg in a heartbeat and been happy for the wheelchair if she could only have had the use of both hands . . . and her face . . . and her voice.

The worst challenge of a disability like hers—perhaps any disability, Edith suspected—was not so much the physical hurdles, but the fact that people around her, even her own daughter and granddaughter, treated her like a slow-witted child, as if paralysis of body equaled senility of mind. Ever since that dreadful night when the EMTs had dragged her back from the brink of eternity, she had been moving in reverse, shrinking, diminishing. The world had turned upside down, and without warning or permission, she had become her daughter's daughter.

True, she couldn't play the piano or wield a sharp knife any longer, or even bake cookies without burning them around the edges. But her mind was every bit as acute as it once was, and she longed for real dialogue rather than the infantile interchanges that masqueraded as conversation. She was certain if she had to answer the question, "How are you feeling today?" one more time, she might run screaming from the room—except that she could neither run nor scream.

Abby turned from the cutting board at the sink and tossed a handful of tomato wedges into the salad bowl. "How are you feeling today, Mama?" she asked.

Edith tried to arch her eyebrows and roll her eyes, but only one side arched and rolled, and she was pretty sure the effect was lost on her daughter. "Fine."

Abby sat down opposite her at the table. "Look, Mama, I know how difficult this is for you—"

As if, Edith thought, borrowing one of her granddaughter's favorite phrases.

"I know you'd love nothing more than to be back here in the kitchen, cooking meals for us, the way you always did before you had the—well, you know. Before."

Before the stroke, Edith's mind supplied.

You can say the word without shocking me. I live with it every day.

"Anyway," Abby went on, "I wish you could do all those things, too. But I worry about you. I don't want you to get hurt. You're my responsibility; I have to take care of you. And I can't always be here to keep an eye on you. Do you understand?"

I ought to, Edith thought. *If I'm not mistaken, this is a verbatim repetition of a lecture I gave you once—oh, about forty-five years ago.* But it was simpler to give in than to attempt an argument. "Yes."

"All right, then. We have an agreement?"

Edith gave a lopsided nod. "Yes."

"Good. Because I need to be able to go to work without expecting the fire department or the police to come calling at my office."

I get it, I get it. Enough, already, Edith's mind shot back.

Abby glanced at the clock over the sink. "Dinner will be ready in about half an hour. I think I'll get out of these pantyhose and heels. My feet are killing me."

Edith laid a hand on her daughter's arm. "Wait," she tried to say. "We've got thirty minutes to ourselves. Can't we talk?"

But the words came out garbled, and Abby misunderstood, or was only half listening. "Talk?" She smiled and patted Edith's hand. "I know. It's hard for you to talk. That's OK. I understand."

And then she was gone, leaving Edith alone to concentrate on tearing the lettuce into little pieces.

⁓

Dinner was a sullen, silent affair, with Neal Grace offering little except to complain about the chicken pasta.

"I understand T. J. came home with you after school," Abby said, working hard to assume a pleasant tone.

"Yeah. So what?"

"It wasn't an indictment, Neal Grace. It's called conversation."

"Right." Her daughter raised her head and pushed her hair out of her eyes. "OK, here's some conversation for you. How about calling me 'Neal,' like I've asked you to a hundred times, instead of 'Neal Grace'? It makes me sound like a baby, or some kind of redneck."

Abby sighed. "I'll try, I'll try."

Neal Grace glared at her. "Fine."

"Fine," Abby repeated.

But she couldn't just leave it at that. Something was wrong with her daughter, and she felt compelled—or at the very least, obligated—to find out what it was.

"Neal Grace—excuse me. *Neal.* What's bothering you, honey? If you need to talk, you know—"

"If I needed to talk, I'd be talking, now wouldn't I?" Neal countered. "Nothing's wrong. Just drop it, OK?"

"Is everything all right at school?"

"School's fine." She finished off a tomato wedge and looked around the table. "Is there any more salad?"

"A little, I think. You haven't touched your pasta."

"I don't want it." Neal got up, went to the kitchen, and returned with the big wooden bowl.

"What do you mean you don't want it? It's your favorite."

Neal rolled her eyes. "It's got chicken. I'm a vegetarian."

"Since when?" Abby cast a glance at Mama, who had a bit of pasta sauce dripping down her chin. She leaned over and wiped her mother's mouth with her own napkin, then turned back to Neal.

"Since—I don't know. Since now." Neal scraped the last of the romaine onto her salad plate. "Eating meat is cruel to animals."

"You're kidding, right?" Abby laughed, trying to lighten the mood. "The original cheeseburger girl is giving up meat? Now, that's a switch."

"Maybe it's time for a change," Neal said. She finished her salad and tossed her napkin on the table. "May I be excused?"

"Don't you want dessert? There's ice cream, and Granny Q made cookies this afternoon."

"They're burned," Neal muttered, avoiding her grandmother's eyes. "Besides, I've got homework."

She bolted for the stairs before Abby could say another word.

Edith followed Abby to the kitchen and watched while she put away the leftovers, made a pot of decaf, and loaded the dishes in the dishwasher. It was no use trying to help. Abby wouldn't let her do anything, anyway.

"It's a nice night," Abby said when the kitchen was clean. "How about if we take our coffee out on the porch?"

They went outside and settled themselves, Edith in the chaise lounge and Abby in the swing that hung suspended from the rafters. The street was quiet, and through the tops of the trees they could see a few stars in the dark sky. From somewhere in the distance, music drifted on the night air.

"It's a little chilly out here. Do you want a sweater?"

Edith shook her head, but Abby got up anyway and went into the house. She came back with a sweater and the small lap-sized afghan from the back of the sofa. She draped the sweater around Edith's shoulders and patted her on the back. "That's better, isn't it?"

Sure, Edith thought. *You're cold, so I have to put on a sweater.* She shrugged it away from her shoulders and let it drop onto the back of the chaise. Abby, not to be outdone, left the swing for a second time and readjusted it.

For a long time they sat in silence, sipping at their coffee and listening to the sounds of birds rustling in the trees and the distant music. On just such a glorious evening, Edith recalled, Sam Long had sat on this very porch and proposed to her—probably with Mother and Daddy peering out at them from behind the curtains. On a thousand such evenings, she and Sam had snuggled together in the swing he had built himself, talking and laughing and planning together until the mantel clock struck midnight. And until recently, she and her daughter had spent countless hours on this same porch, deep in conversation about Abby's photography and the people John Mac helped and Neal Grace's successes and failures.

If only they could talk that way again.

Abby sighed. "I don't know what to do about Neal Grace," she said. "I feel as if I don't even know my own daughter anymore. What on earth is going on with her?"

Edith's heart leaped, and she turned toward her daughter to respond, to discuss the child they both loved, to try to find a solution—together. But then Abby went on musing, and Edith clamped her mouth shut again. Abby wasn't talking to her. She was simply rambling to herself.

"That music," Abby said. "It reminds me of a man I met today up on Pack Square. A fiddler named Devin Connor. Kind of a mountain man, I guess. At least that's the kind of music he plays. He didn't seem to have much—I don't suppose he would, if he's fiddling on the streets for quarters. But there was something about him, something intriguing. He was so gentle and kind. And I never met anyone with so much passion for his music. He played 'Twinkle, Twinkle, Little Star' for a toddler in a stroller and had that child absolutely entranced. I have an appointment to interview him tomorrow for the magazine. I can't wait to find out what makes him tick . . ."

Edith laid her head back against the cushion of the chaise and stared at the stars as her daughter's voice continued to wash over her. Clearly Abby didn't expect a response. She rarely had the patience to wait for one these days.

The music came down from somewhere in the hills and seeped into Edith's soul. And in the sky and the stars and the music, she

found herself drawn close—very close indeed—to that place where time meets eternity and the man she loved beckoned to her
from the other side.

6

What Makes Devin Tick

At eleven the next morning, Abby was bending over the layout table, drowning in proof pages, when she looked up to see Ford Hambrick standing in the doorway with a cat-caught-the-canary grin on his face. "You've got company."

"Company?" Abby frowned. "I don't have time for company. Who is it? Birdie again? Tell her I can't see her now, but I'll call her tonight."

"It's not Birdie." He arched one eyebrow in a rakish expression. "It's a *man.*"

"A what?"

"A man. You know—tall, tanned, good-looking. Says you asked to interview him."

"Devin Connor?"

"Exactly. From the look on your face, I gather you know who he is?"

"Yes, of course." Abby took a deep breath

in an effort to return her heartbeat to normal. Her mind recalled the echoes of his music and the glint of intensity in his clear blue eyes.

She straightened up and ran a hand through her hair. "Take him into the conference room, will you, Ford? Get him coffee—or whatever he wants—and tell him I'll be with him in a minute."

"You got it, Boss." Ford disappeared, and Abby looked frantically around the cluttered office. Where was her tape recorder? And her camera. She'd need her camera.

Annoyed with herself for getting so flustered, she rooted in her desk and came up with her palm-sized recorder, a legal pad, and a pen. She hefted her camera bag onto her shoulder and headed out the door.

The conference room, the largest room in the suite of offices leased by *Carolina Monthly,* doubled as a staff kitchen. The middle of the room was dominated by a large rectangular table surrounded by chairs. In the far corner, a more intimate seating area offered a sofa, two easy chairs, and a coffee table, and on the left-hand wall an arrangement of cabinets held a coffee maker, a small refrigerator, and a sink.

When Abby entered the room, Devin

Connor was standing with his back to her, stirring sugar into a stoneware mug bearing the Asheville logo and a design of blue and purple mountains. She hadn't remembered him being so tall. Six-two, at least, and wearing blue jeans with a carefully ironed collarless white shirt. A well-worn brown leather jacket hung on the back of one of the conference chairs.

She plunked her camera bag onto the table, and he turned.

"Mr. Connor," she said briskly, moving toward him with her hand outstretched. "I'm Abby McDougall. We met yesterday."

"I remember," he said in a deep voice that just hinted at amusement. "I'm here, after all."

Abby felt her neck grow hot. "Well, thank you for coming, Mr. Connor."

"Devin," he corrected.

She inclined her head. "Devin. My assistant got you some coffee, I see. Do you need anything else?"

He smiled. "Not at the moment."

"Fine. Fine." Abby cringed as she heard her own voice pitched half an octave above normal. She cleared her throat. "Shall we sit down?"

Devin pulled out the chair at the head of the table and waited until Abby settled herself, then took the seat at a right angle to her. "I'm not exactly certain why you wanted to interview me," he said with a chuckle. "I'm simply a fiddler who plays music on the streets. I doubt that's very interesting to anyone."

"It's interesting to me," Abby blurted out, then corrected herself. "To our readers, I mean." She found herself staring at him—at those blue eyes, and the recalcitrant lock of sun-streaked hair that fell over his forehead. At his tanned face with the smile lines that fanned out from the corners of his eyes. At his fingers, long and lean and squared off at the tips, with clean, well-cut nails.

He seemed perfectly composed, sitting there with his hands wrapped around his coffee cup. Not nervous or the least bit uneasy. Contentment radiated from him, and her mind summed him up in a single sentence: *Here is a man at peace with himself and his life.*

Seeing him up close, she also realized that he was younger than she had originally assumed. Mid to late forties, perhaps. Quite handsome in an outdoorsy sort of way. He was clean and neatly dressed, his beard and hair professionally trimmed. *This is no mountain man,* she said to herself.

Her mind, unbidden, finished the thought: *But he is a man. Definitely a man.*

Abby pushed the notion aside. She'd best get down to business—and quickly.

She centered the legal pad on the table in front of her, laid the tape recorder between them, and looked up. "Do you mind if I tape our interview? I'll take notes as well, but I like to make sure I cover all the bases," she said, sliding into her role of professional journalist.

"Of course."

"All right, then." She pushed the red button on the side of the machine and checked to make sure the tape was running. "Now, Mr. Connor, let's start with the basics. You are—how old?"

"Please, call me Devin," he repeated. "I'm forty-eight."

"And you live—"

"Here, near Asheville. I have a cabin up in the mountains."

Abby smiled to herself. A cabin. In the mountains. Maybe he was a mountain man after all.

"Do you have—" She paused. "A family?"

"I did, once," he said. "They're gone now. I'd rather not talk about them, if you don't mind." He took a sip of coffee and looked at her. "And what about you? Husband? Children?"

"I live with my teenage daughter and an elderly mother."

"No husband?"

For a split second Abby hesitated, exasperation rising up within her. Who was doing the interviewing here, anyway? Then she stifled her irritation and answered, "I'm a widow. My husband died two years ago."

"I'm sorry to hear that. It must be difficult for you," he said, leaning slightly forward, as though he might reach out a hand in sympathy.

The sincere starkness of his words were a sharp contrast to the myriad of platitudes and pat responses she had received after John Mac's death. This man did sound as if he genuinely understood the difficulties she faced.

But Abby didn't want the interview detoured. She steered the conversation back to him. "I'd like to know—that is, I think our readers would be interested in what motivates you to play your music on the street," she said. "You're very good, you know. Maybe even good enough to do this professionally. But you can't possibly make a living on the donations people give you."

"I don't care about making a living," Devin answered. "I care about making a *life*. Music is life to me. It's love. You don't sell love; you give it away. You lift it up as an offering, and you are enriched whether the world affirms it or not."

Abby scribbled his words on the pad, just to make certain she got them right. She could almost see the article now, perhaps with a cover spread. The mountain philosopher. The fiddler of life. Her mind spun with the possibilities.

"Tell me more about yourself," she said, shifting back in her chair. "About your background. How you live. What generates such passion for your music."

"I have a better idea," he said. "Let me show you."

Never in all her fifty-one years had Abby ridden on a motorcycle, nor had she desired to do so. Every year, when the Honda Hoot rolled into town, she cursed the clogged traffic and the noise and the exhaust. Motorcycles were nasty, dangerous machines ridden by anarchists and hippie throwbacks. Now she swallowed down another of her preconceived notions and held on for dear life.

Devin's bike wasn't a motorcycle, technically. It was an Italian-made scooter, silvery-blue. "I have an old pickup truck, too," he said, "but I prefer to ride this when the weather's nice." He handed her a helmet. "It's a Vespa. A classic."

The wind whipped her face as they headed down 240, out Old Charlotte Highway, and up into the hills south of town. Once she got over her initial terror, the experience reminded Abby of younger days when she had owned an ancient Triumph Spitfire convertible. That long-forgotten sense of freedom washed over her again, and she laughed out loud.

Devin turned and smiled over his shoulder at her. "Great, isn't it?" he yelled.

Abby laughed again and clutched tighter to the leather of his jacket. Her life was still the same, with all its stress and struggle and loneliness and frustration. But somehow, from the back of a little blue motor scooter, everything felt different. With the wind coursing around her and the mountains before her and the glorious clear sky bright above her, she could almost see light and color washing over her world again.

A mile or two past the entrance to the Parkway, Devin slowed the scooter and turned left, and they began to wind up a long paved road. At a break in the trees, she looked down and saw that they were very high. The city spread out below them like a toy town, remote in the distance.

The scooter kept climbing. The road narrowed and turned to gravel. Tall trees on either side tangled their branches overhead to make a living arch, a tunnel of green. And then, just when Abby was beginning to think they had no choice but to crest the ridge and come down on the other side, Devin veered right into a clearing and killed the engine.

"We're here." He slid off the seat, removed his helmet, and helped Abby to dismount. "Did you enjoy the ride?"

"My legs are still vibrating, but yes, I liked it very much." She smiled up at him. "Where are we?"

"This is where I live."

Abby looked around. It was a tranquil, stunning location, totally secluded. Just up the hill, a log cabin blended into the surrounding scenery as if it had grown organically out of the mountainside. Behind it, the ridge shot up steeply, heavily wooded and studded with huge boulders. To the right, the land leveled off in an open stretch of pasture before plunging downhill again. A rushing stream, dammed with rocks to create a small waterfall, splashed and sparkled into a pond. Two deer browsing at the edge of the water lifted their heads in curiosity.

For a moment Abby felt as if she had stepped into another world, another time. The clearing was absolutely silent. There was no sound of civilization, not even the distant white noise of cars passing by on the highway.

She listened again. No. It wasn't silent. She could make out the calling of birds and the rustle of small animals in the woods—squirrels, perhaps, or rabbits. A hawk soared overhead and disappeared beyond the tree line. And underneath it all, she heard the rush of water cascading down the mountain into the pond, and out again in a small cataract on the other side.

"This is so beautiful," she said, and found herself whispering. It seemed a sacrilege to intrude on such beauty.

The idea startled her. Abby hadn't given much thought to the idea of holiness—indeed, to anything spiritual—in a very long time. And yet the presence of God, or at least the presence of something deeply loving and peaceful and sacred, clearly permeated this place. *This,* a voice in the back of her mind murmured, *is what heaven must be like.*

And yet something didn't quite fit. They couldn't be more than fifteen minutes from town. Abby's mind retraced the route they had taken. By her figuring, they must be near the top of the ridge that backed up to the Blue Ridge Parkway. This was a prime location, and very expensive—the kind of land developers purchased for gated communities of half-million-dollar homes. Not the kind of property owned by a street musician who had no visible means of support.

"Come on," Devin was saying. "Let's sit on the porch and talk. I'll make us some lunch."

She followed him to the cabin and settled into one of the big oak rockers on the covered porch that faced out over the valley and the mountains to the west. Leaving the front door wide open, Devin went into the kitchen. She could hear him puttering around, humming to himself as he worked.

Abby waited. A medium-sized dog—a cross between a beagle and a shelty, she guessed—appeared at the side of the porch and came up to investigate. She extended her hand to be sniffed, then rubbed his ears. "What's the dog's name?" she asked through the open doorway.

Devin poked his head around the corner and looked. "That's Rachmaninoff," he said. "Rocky for short. Mozart's around somewhere. He'll show up as soon as he gets wind of the food."

Sure enough, the moment Devin reappeared with a tray bearing sandwiches and tall glasses of iced tea, a sweet-faced golden retriever came barreling up from behind the pond and plopped down expectantly at his master's knee. "He's a real lover," Devin said, "but a terrible beggar."

Devin served her a lunch of chicken salad sandwiches on homemade bread. A simple meal, and yet Abby had not tasted anything so good in months. They ate quietly, with Abby sneaking a couple of bread crusts to Mozart when Devin wasn't looking. After a while she gathered her courage to ask the questions that were pressing in on her.

"This place is so . . . secluded," she said. "There must be a lot of undeveloped acreage surrounding the cabin."

Devin nodded. "About sixty-five acres, give or take. The property runs from the main road all the way up to the crest of the ridge."

She looked past him into the cabin. It appeared to be one large room, with a kitchen divided from the main room by an island, and a loft overhead. Beyond the kitchen, on the far side, she could see a closed door. A bedroom, perhaps?

Abby set her tea glass on the small table between the rockers. "Do you mind if I use your rest room?"

"Be my guest. Through the bedroom door, on the left."

"Thanks." Abby didn't really need to use the facilities, but she was uncontrollably curious about how Devin Connor lived.

What she found inside his cabin surprised her. It was, as she had suspected, basically one large open space, but crafted with meticulous care. To her right as she entered, a compact kitchen formed an L, with a cooking bar set at an angle to the corner. On the opposite wall, a huge stone fireplace rose up into the vaulted ceiling, surrounded by a brown leather sofa and several comfortable-looking overstuffed chairs. In one corner stood a baby grand piano littered with staff paper.

She crossed the room and opened the door. The bedroom, although not large, was decorated in soothing tones of dark green and burgundy, and furnished with an iron bed neatly covered with a handmade quilt. An oval area rug covered much of the wood floor, and in one corner a cozy sitting area had been created—a mission oak library table topped with a Tiffany lamp stood between two dark green easy chairs.

"I'll say one thing for him—he's got good taste," Abby muttered as she pushed the bathroom door ajar. The bath, nearly as large as the bedroom, was tiled in forest green with burgundy accents and dominated by a double-size shower encased in glass bricks.

She washed her hands, took a last longing look at the glorious shower, then wandered slowly back through the bedroom and out into the main living area. Devin Connor might claim to be a simple man, but this home was no rustic mountain cabin. Anyone who played a fiddle for quarters on the street couldn't afford luxuries like leather sofas and a baby grand.

She returned to the porch and resumed her seat in the rocking chair. "You have a nice house, Devin," she said.

He lifted his eyebrows and gazed at her. "And you're wondering how a penniless street musician can manage sixty-five acres and a log cabin with leather furniture and a glass block shower."

Abby ducked her head. "It crossed my mind, yes. A place like this—" She waved a hand at the cabin and the stunning vista spread out before them.

"What makes you think I own it?"

Abby looked at him and saw once again that hint of amusement in his clear blue eyes, that almost-smile that played about his lips. Her heart did a little flip-flop. "This property doesn't belong to you?"

"You're the reporter. What do your instincts tell you?"

She thought a minute. "I'd guess that—well, maybe you have friends in high places. And you're looking after this property for them . . . like a caretaker."

He pushed the hair back from his forehead and stared out across the pond. "Yes," he said after a moment. "Exactly like a caretaker."

Abby glanced at her watch. It was nearly two. "Devin, I appreciate your bringing me up here. And I'd like to get to know you better—" The words came out before she could censor them, and she scrambled to explain. "For the article, I mean. But at the moment I really need to get back to the office. I've been gone too long."

"Right," he said, getting to his feet. "I ought to get to work myself." He took the lunch tray back into the cabin and returned with his battered black fiddle case. "But before we go, I'd like to respond to one of your questions." He opened the case, retrieved his fiddle and bow, and sat down on the top step of the porch. "You asked earlier what generates my passion for music." He waved the bow at the far mountains. "There's your answer."

He began to play, a lilting, haunting melody. A ballad, Abby thought, although she couldn't identify the tune. The music soared into the bright afternoon air, wove through the trees, and reverberated back from the mountainside. With a gentle plaintiveness, the notes worked their way into Abby's heart and stirred within her the longing for—

For what?

She didn't know. But the music called to her, reaching some empty, tender spot hidden within her. The touch hurt, but it was a bittersweet pain. A nostalgic yearning, a deep homesickness of the soul.

Without a single word, the music spoke to her of love and risk and new beginnings, of wishes granted and yet to come, of beauty far beyond her own understanding.

And when it ceased, she had a glimpse—perhaps for the first time in her life—of the kind of passion that drove Devin Connor to give his music freely to the world.

7

Metamorphosis

"Neal! Thurmond's coming!"

Neal turned to see the bathroom door partially open, with T. J. Sweet's head poked through the crack. She grinned. As her best friend, T. J. always watched her back, but sometimes she went a little overboard with the bodyguard routine.

"So what? That little toad of a principal wouldn't be caught dead coming into the girls' bathroom. He's scared spitless that somebody might slap a sexual harassment lawsuit on him. Shut the door."

T. J. came into the room and let the door close behind her. "What's gotten into you, Neal? If he nails you for smoking, you'll be suspended. Not the best way to start out your senior year."

Neal waved the cigarette at the mirror and gazed at her reflection through the smoke. "My point exactly. This is my senior year, and I intend to make the most of it. Now, what do you think of this outfit?"

T. J. stared at Neal as if seeing her for the first time. "Where did you get that? You look like a hooker."

"Exactly." Neal straightened one sleeve of the tight black sweater and pushed the waist of her leather miniskirt down below her bellybutton. "It's time for some changes, my friend. Michael Damatto won't be able to resist me in this outfit."

"Mike Damatto? That biker who rides the red Harley and works at the garage?"

"He's not just a biker," Neal shot back. "He's . . . complex."

"He's wild, you mean. And he's twenty-three."

Neal turned toward T. J. and shook her head. "Since when did you turn into the Church Lady? You sound like my grand-mother."

"I just want to graduate, OK? And your grandmother would drop dead on the spot if she saw you dressed like that."

"She's not going to see me. I'm meeting Mike in exactly"—she looked at her watch—"fifteen minutes."

"In fifteen minutes we'll be ten minutes into Lit class, remember? And if—"

A banging on the door interrupted them. The principal's wheedling voice came through the closed door. "Miss Sweet, I know you're in there. Open up."

T. J. opened the door a crack. Neal could see Thurmond's round, red face on the other side. The veins in his neck bulged against his collar, and he tugged at his tie as if he were choking.

"Is something wrong, Mr. Thurmond?" T. J. asked in a high-pitched childish sing-song.

"I . . . I thought I saw Miss McDougall come in here," he stammered, sniffing the air like a dog trying to catch a scent. "Has someone been smoking?"

"Smoking?" T. J. said in her best innocent tone. "Why, I don't know, Mr. Thurmond. Surely not. This is school property, after all. Smoking is strictly forbidden."

"Indeed it is," he huffed. "What about Miss McDougall?"

"Yes, sir, she's here with me." T. J. leaned closer to him. "We've got a little problem, sir."

"Problem? What kind of problem?"

"Nothing serious. Just a little"—she lowered her voice to a whisper—"female thing. Neal Grace was—well, caught unawares, if you catch my drift."

Thurmond jerked back as if he'd been snakebit, and his face turned from its normal red to a shade somewhere between fuchsia and purple. Neal escaped into one of the stalls, overcome with laughter.

"Oh. Well . . . ah, yes. I see," the principal said. "Take your time, both of you. No rush. No rush at all." He disappeared, and Neal could hear his wing tips on the stairs as he bolted for the safety of his office.

She came out of the stall and gave T. J. a high-five. "That was brilliant! Total genius! Thanks so much. I gotta go."

"Go? Go where?"

"I told you, Teej, I'm meeting Mike Damatto. He's probably waiting for me behind the gym right now. I'm going to be late."

"But what about Lit class?"

Neal laughed. "I'm ditching Lit, of course. And Biology. *And* Study Hall. See you tomorrow."

"Tomorrow?" T. J. frowned. "But—"

"Gotta run. Oh, by the way, I'm leaving a

message for Mom telling her I'm having dinner at your house and studying with you
tonight. If she calls, cover for me, OK? I'll
come by later and tell you all about it."

"This is not a good idea."

Neal ran a hand through her hair. "This is
my one big chance with Mike Damatto, T. J.
Believe me, it's a very good idea."

⁓

The bar was dark and smoky, and the beer
was lukewarm. Neal didn't really like beer,
but Mike had brought it to the table, so she
sipped at it and pretended to be enjoying
herself. In one corner, a jukebox was playing a morose country song, its rhythms
punctuated by the clack of pool balls from
the next room.

"So," Mike said as he wiped his mouth on
the back of his hand, "pretty cool place,
huh?"

Neal looked around. "Yeah, it's great."

It wasn't great. Not even close. Every
time Neal moved her feet, her shoes stuck
to the floor. And she didn't even want to
think about what kind of unidentified protein
might be lurking amid the chips or chopped
up in the salsa. Her beer glass had an old

lipstick stain on the rim, and she gingerly turned it around to drink from the other side.

The place was a dive, but that didn't matter. She was on a date with Mike Damatto. He had a face to die for, and a body to match. Muscled arms. Great abs. A square jaw and a shock of dark hair that punked up over his forehead. His eyelids drooped perpetually at half-mast—what T. J. called "bedroom eyes." Now those eyes were watching her with a smoldering intensity as he drank his beer and ordered another.

The tattoo on his right forearm—a snake coiled to strike—had a banner below it that read, *Dangerous.* But he wasn't, Neal thought. Or maybe just a *little* dangerous. She had to admit that danger was what had drawn her to him in the first place.

Neal had always been exactly what her family expected her to be—a good student, honest, respectful. But since her father's death and, more recently, her grandmother's stroke, something dark and troubling brewed inside her, an anger she couldn't articulate. She felt as if she might explode at any moment.

Dad was gone. Mom was always busy.

Granny Q was of no use to anyone. She couldn't take it anymore.

And then she met Mike.

Their initial meeting back in July had been purely coincidental, although Mike insisted on referring to it as "good karma." She had picked up T. J. and the two of them were headed for the stadium to take in a Saturday afternoon baseball game. Neither of them liked baseball, and Asheville's minor league team, the Tourists, was having a pretty miserable season. But a friend of T. J.'s from another school had promised to hook them up with a couple of cute guys.

Neal had just turned the corner a block from the stadium and was looking for a place to park when the oil light on the dashboard flashed red. She knew enough about engines to realize this was bad news, so she immediately pulled into the garage on the corner and turned off the engine.

A mechanic sauntered out. The patch on his grease-covered overalls read, *Mike*. He looked them over and grinned. "We close at two on Saturday," he said, glancing at his watch. "But if you've got an emergency—"

"The oil light came on," Neal said as she got out of the car. She turned to T. J. "You go on ahead and meet Katie and the guys. I'll call Mom and catch up with you later."

"You sure?" T. J. frowned. "I can stay with you."

"Yeah, go on. Maybe this won't take too long."

Neal watched as T. J. set off on foot in the direction of the stadium, and when she turned back, she found Mike staring at her.

"What are you looking at?" she demanded.

"Nothin'," he drawled. "Nothin' but the girl of my dreams." He raised one eyebrow. "Oil light, you said?"

The problem with the oil light turned out to be a short in the electrical system. In thirty minutes Mike had it fixed and was closing up the shop. While she phoned her mother to get a credit card number to pay him, he washed up and stripped off the coveralls to reveal an awesome buff body in black jeans and a black sleeveless T-shirt. She couldn't take her eyes off the snake tattoo on his upper arm, the way it writhed when his muscles flexed.

"You can leave your car parked here while you go to the game," he said. "Or you can take a ride with me and we can get acquainted." He pointed toward a red Harley with bright chrome parked at the side of the building.

Neal hesitated. "They won't miss me for a while," she said at last.

They roared through town on Mike's motorcycle, detoured to the drive-through window at Backyard Burgers and bought Cokes, then went to the park and sat at a shaded picnic table. Neal told him about her father's death and her grandmother's stroke—the first time she had been able to confess those feelings to anyone. Mike talked about how his father had abused both him and his mother and then abandoned them, and how his mom had worked herself to death trying to make ends meet. Despite everything, he said, he was determined to be a success. He was saving money to buy out the owner of the garage.

"My father would have helped you," Neal said. "That's what he did—helped people start their own businesses."

"I coulda used his help." Mike shrugged. "Now that Mom's gone, I don't really have anybody who believes in me."

The words came out of Neal's mouth before she had time to think about them: "I could believe in you, Mike."

"I'd like that," he said. "I'd like that a lot." Every chance she got all during July and early August, Neal had dropped by the garage to talk to Mike. His boss called her "jailbait" and tried to run her off, but she kept coming back. She couldn't help herself. For a long time after Daddy's death and Granny Q's stroke, she had felt like a zombie, just going through the motions, but her conversations with Mike Damatto made her feel like a real person. He liked her. He needed her. And now—maybe thanks to the miniskirt and new hairdo—he was beginning to regard her with a different kind of interest.

She knew her mother would not approve. But she was seventeen—old enough to know what she wanted. Old enough to make her own decisions. And apparently, if the expression on Mike's face was any indication, old enough to attract a real man rather than the stupid, immature high-school boys her mother thought she went out with.

Something nagged at the back of Neal's mind. A warning. Questions she couldn't— or didn't want to—answer. Why Mike? Why now? Did she really want him, or did she only want something different?

She pushed the questions aside. Mike was staring at her, his eyes dark and brooding.

"So," he said, "you want to get out of here? Go somewhere?"

"Like where?"

He shrugged. "I don't know. My place, maybe?" His mouth turned up in a slow, seductive grin.

She stubbed out her cigarette, forced down the last swallow of beer, and got unsteadily to her feet.

"Sure," she said. "Why not?"

8

Prospects

Abby awoke to the soothing caress of music—an elusive, lyrical tune—and was vaguely aware that the melody had threaded through her dreams. But it was only the sound of rain splashing against the windowpane.

The music of the rain reminded her of Devin Connor. It had been almost a week since she had met with him. On Monday, after their initial interview the previous Friday, she had revisited Café on the Square in hopes of finding him playing in the plaza. Yesterday she had invented another reason to go to Pack Square, but still no Devin. And today was a lost cause. Surely he would not be out in this weather, playing his fiddle in the rain.

She had tried to telephone him, but without success. Every time she had called, she had gotten his answering machine and then hung up without leaving a message. What could she possibly say—"I can't stop thinking about you"? Absurd. And she couldn't make up an excuse about needing more information for the article—not when she hadn't even begun to put it together.

She'd just have to be patient. Besides, she had other things to do with her time and attention than obsess about Devin Connor. Mama seemed so discouraged and withdrawn, and Abby had no idea what to do about it. Neal, fortunately, had been in better spirits the past few days. She was spending a lot of time at T. J.'s, but Abby couldn't fault her for wanting to escape the oppression of this house. Besides, T. J. was a good kid. Maybe Abby was expecting too much, wanting Neal to confide in her rather than in her best friend. The important thing was that Neal Grace had someone to talk to, a friend who would be supportive and encouraging.

Abby only wished *she* had someone to talk to, someone who could understand. On the subject of Devin Connor, Birdie was no help at all.

She remembered that fleeting sense of

freedom she had felt when riding on the back of Devin's motor scooter, that tantalizing combination of serenity and longing she had tasted in the time she had spent at his cabin.

She pushed the thought firmly from her mind. Devin might be something of a mystery, and mysteries were always compelling. But he was also an idealistic dreamer who made ends meet by living as a caretaker on someone else's property.

Abby made the bed and went into the bathroom. She had just stepped out of the shower when she heard the phone ringing. She waited. Neal didn't answer it, and Mama never would. Still dripping wet and muttering to herself about teenagers, she wrapped a towel around herself, dashed into the bedroom, and picked up the receiver.

"Abby?" Birdie's voice said. "Are you all right? You sound out of breath."

"I was in the shower."

"Oops, sorry." Birdie laughed. "I was just calling to remind you about dinner tonight. Six-thirty, our place. Assuming the rain stops, Taylor's going to grill out, so dress casually."

"Dinner?" Abby repeated. "Tonight?"

"Yes, tonight. It's Thursday, remember? You're supposed to meet Charles."

Abby rubbed at her eyes with a corner of the towel. "Who's Charles?"

"Charles Bingham. *Doctor* Charles Bingham. The new business prof at WNCU." An exasperated sigh whooshed through the earpiece. "I invited you last week, the day we went to lunch. Come on, Abby. Fifty-three, good-looking, single. Does this ring any bells?"

"Oh." Abby frowned. "I don't know, Birdie, I—"

"No excuses. Forget it. You are not going to bail on me. You promised."

Abby gave up. She didn't really have a good excuse to beg off, and arguing with Birdie was always a waste of breath and energy. "All right. What's the time again?"

"Six-thirty. Bring a salad."

"I'll be there. Under duress, mind you."

"Atta girl." Birdie laughed. "See you tonight. Love you. Bye."

Abby hung up the phone, started to sink down onto the bed, then remembered she was still wet and jumped up again. The last thing she wanted to do tonight was go out on a blind date and have to be charming. But Birdie was unstoppable once she had her mind made up. Better simply to brace herself, meet this Charles Bingham, and get it over with.

Charles, as it turned out, wasn't so bad.

"So, what do you think?" Birdie hissed in her ear as she dragged Abby into the kitchen on the pretense of needing help serving dessert.

Abby leaned against the island in the middle of the kitchen. "I think he's very nice."

"Very *nice?*" Birdie shook her head. "The last time you used that line was in high school, and the boy was some pimply-faced nerd who carried a slide rule jammed down the back of his pants. Don't mess with me. Do you like him?"

"Yes," Abby said. "I like him very much. He seems . . . stable."

Birdie shook her head. "Stable."

"Is there an echo in here?" Abby thoroughly enjoyed yanking Birdie's chain, but she could see from her friend's expression that she was not amused. "OK, I'll be serious. You didn't oversell him. He's handsome, in a mature, professorial sort of way. He's an above-average listener and carries on a decent conversation. He's got a sense of humor. I'd prefer he didn't talk quite so much about the prospects of the stock market, but—"

"But you like him."

"I already said that, didn't I? I like him, OK?" She picked up a dessert fork from the counter and held it high, in imitation of Sally Field at the Academy Awards. "I like him! I really, really like him!"

"Good." Birdie turned her back and began spooning coffee grounds into the basket. "Because you've got another date with him next week."

Abby balked. "What?"

"He's going to ask you to go with him to the faculty banquet next Friday night."

"And you know this *how?*"

Birdie turned and grinned. "Because he told Taylor while they were out on the patio grilling the steaks."

"Did he leave a note in your locker, too?" Abby grimaced. "I'm not sure I'm ready for this."

"Of course you are." Birdie laid out four

slices of pound cake and nodded toward the fridge. "Get the strawberries, will you? And the bowl of whipped cream."

"Listen, Birdie—"

Birdie turned and pointed the cake knife in Abby's direction. "*You* listen. It's time for you to start dating again, and you're not likely to find anyone half as eligible as Charles Bingham. Besides, he *really, really likes you.*"

Abby began to sling strawberries onto the cake. "Oh, are you psychic now?"

"No, I'm observant. Anyone with eyes could see it. The way he looks at you, the way he leans forward when he's talking—"

"You'll have me walking down the aisle next."

The coffee was done. Birdie reached for the pot. "And what's so horrible about that idea?"

"Nothing." Abby paused with a scoop of whipped cream in midair. "It's just that—" Tears clogged her throat.

Setting the coffeepot back on the warmer, Birdie came to Abby's side of the island and put her arms around her. "I know. You still miss John Mac," she said quietly. "You can't imagine being with anyone else."

She stroked Abby's back with the flat of her hand. "Just give Charles a chance, will you? You had a wonderful marriage. There's no reason you couldn't have another one."

Abby took a paper napkin from the holder and dabbed at her eyes. "You're right. John Mac would want me to be happy, I know. Still, it's hard to let go."

"Of course it is. But it's time to start."

Abby nodded. "All right. You win. Just promise me one thing."

"Anything."

"Promise me you won't push. Let me do this my way, on my timetable."

"I promise," Birdie said. "Cross my heart."

Abby narrowed her eyes. "Why don't I believe you?"

"Because I'm your best friend, and you know me too well?" She grinned. "Meet me after work tomorrow. I'll help you buy a new dress for the banquet."

Abby burst out laughing. "Don't you think we should wait until he actually *asks* me?"

"What a ridiculous notion." Birdie poured the coffee and set the cups on the dessert tray. "He'll ask. Trust me. I know these things."

"Apparently, you know *everything*," Abby muttered under her breath.

"Of course I do. It's my job." She picked up the tray and motioned for Abby to follow.

Abby laughed. "Must be a terrible burden, being right all the time."

"It's a curse." Birdie grinned back at her as she shouldered her way through the door into the dining room. "But we all make do with the crosses we have to bear."

9

Mothers and Daughters

Quinn House
September

Neal looked in the mirror and pushed her hair into spikes, making the ends stand up straight over the cowlick in the back. Perfect. She grinned at her reflection and twisted her torso for a better view of the tattoo on her right shoulder. A small red heart with a dagger thrust through it. The swelling had gone down, and most of the pain had subsided.

It was only a small tattoo, but that wouldn't make any difference to Mom. She would be furious if she found out. But she wasn't going to see it—not if Neal had anything to say about it. Besides, Neal was almost eighteen; she could do whatever she wanted.

"My body, my life," she muttered under her breath. She zipped up her jeans, slipped on a black T-shirt, and pulled her heaviest denim jacket out of the closet. Today was going to be great. A shiver of excitement raced through her. Mike had the whole day off, and he'd convinced her to skip school and ride with him up to a friend's cabin in the mountains. T. J. would undoubtedly give her a lecture about missing the History midterm, but so far she had been great about covering for Neal, and she wouldn't rat on her now.

Besides, Mom was so busy these days she probably wouldn't even notice Neal was gone. For nearly a month her mother had been going out two or three times a week with that Charles guy. One night she had even invited him to the house for dinner. Probably a trial run, to see how Neal and Granny Q would take to him.

Neal laughed out loud at the memory of that evening—a total disaster, no matter how you looked at it. The moment Charles entered the house with that bogus grin on his face, she had instantly decided she despised the man. He was the total opposite of Daddy. Neal couldn't imagine what her mother saw in him. He had a shifty look about him, as if he had something to hide, and his smile didn't reach his eyes. Mom gave him a quick tour of Quinn House, and the whole time he seemed to be casing the joint, adding up Mom's net worth on a little calculator inside his head.

Neal couldn't stand him, and the feeling seemed to be mutual. He hadn't said a single word to her the entire evening, just stared at her as if she were some kind of sideshow freak. Granny Q had attempted to talk to him, but he couldn't understand a word she said, and when she passed the gravy, her grip gave way and she dropped it with a big splat, splashing it all over his fifty-dollar silk tie.

Neal had thought the whole situation was pretty funny, but Mom was not amused. When she came back after seeing him to his car, she lit into Neal with a fury, saying that Charles was important to her, and the least her daughter could do was try to be nice to him.

But Neal found it impossible to be nice to someone she didn't trust. And she couldn't talk to Mom about it—not when she was so obviously snowed by the guy. She'd just have to let things take their course and hope old Chuckie would conclude that life with three generations of Quinn women was just too complicated. With any luck, Mom would come to her senses and see through him—or he'd give up and fade away before the relationship got too serious.

But even if Mom didn't dump him—or he didn't dump her—it didn't matter much to Neal. She had her own life now, with Mike Damatto.

She had wished for change, and she had gotten it. When she looked in the mirror these days, she hardly recognized herself. Her hair was cut very short and spiked on the top, and most of the time she dressed all in black. Mom rolled her eyes, and T. J. kept complaining that Neal wasn't herself anymore, but that was exactly what Neal wanted. To be someone else.

She even *felt* different. Mature, like a woman, instead of like a teenager. And that was the way Mike treated her, too.

There were some downsides to her relationship with Mike, of course. She had little in common anymore with her friends at school. Even T. J. seemed to be drifting away, getting more distant. Oh, Teej listened when Neal talked about Mike, and tried to be enthusiastic. But Neal could tell T. J. didn't understand. She couldn't expect her to understand. Teej had never been in love. And she was always so *nervous* about everything. T. J. was sure Neal was going to get into trouble for skipping class, sure her grades would slip, sure her mother would eventually find out and pitch a fit.

But none of that mattered to Neal. What mattered was that she had connected with somebody who loved her—needed her, even. Mike might seem like a tough guy from the outside, but he was really very sensitive.

"Nobody knows me like you," he had said to her the night before when she had sneaked out to meet him. "I don't know what I'd do without you."

"You'd be fine, Mike. Really you would."

She had meant it as an encouragement, but he didn't take it that way. "What do you mean?" he said, pushing away from her. "You promised to stay with me. You're not gonna break that promise, are you?"

"Of course not," she said. "I only meant that you don't need me to be all right. You're good at your job; you're ambitious. You'd be fine, with or without me."

"But I *do* need you," he said. "You don't know how much. You didn't have a father who beat you and then abandoned you. I need somebody who'll never leave me, who'll love me and stand by me no matter what. My life was so empty before you came along. I need you so much, Neal. I'll love you forever. Promise you'll always be here. Promise."

On the one hand, Neal felt warmed and comforted by his declarations of love for her. But she was also aware of a brief surge of annoyance at his possessiveness and insecurity. Still, she reasoned, he'd had a hard life. And now, when he had someone who loved him, it was only natural that he might be a little insecure. She just wished she didn't have to reassure him constantly. She wished he could trust her.

"Promise," he repeated, gripping her shoulders until his fingers pressed painfully into the flesh. "Promise you'll always love me. I couldn't stand it if you left me."

"Mike, you're hurting me!" Tears came, and she tried without success to wrestle out of his grasp.

He released his hold on her. "I'm sorry," he said. "I'm so sorry. I didn't mean to hurt you. I'd never hurt you—you know that, don't you? I love you."

Neal rubbed at the bruises and bit her lip. "Yes, I know," she said. "You didn't mean it."

He stroked her cheek, wiping away the tears. "I'm sorry," he repeated. "But you gotta understand. I love you. I love you so much that it just about makes me crazy when I can't be with you all the time."

"It's all right, Mike," Neal had said. "I love you, too. And I won't leave you. I promise."

As she recalled the events from last night, Neal felt that familiar vacillation of emotions. But she had to admit, it was exciting to have someone who loved her so much and wanted to be with her all the time.

Well, that problem was about to be remedied—for one day, at least. Today Mike would have her all to himself.

She stuffed a few necessities into her backpack, zipped it up, and headed down the stairs. She could hear Mom in the kitchen, talking to Granny Q.

"Come have some breakfast before you go to school, honey," Mom called out.

Neal went into the kitchen and sat down at the table opposite Granny Q. Mom was at the stove flipping pancakes. Neal frowned and cut a questioning glance at her grandmother, who gave a one-sided shrug in response.

"What's the occasion?" Neal said. "You never make pancakes anymore."

Mom leaned across her and put a jug of syrup in the center of the table. "Can't I do something nice for my family without everybody being suspicious?" She smiled and ran a hand through Neal's punked hair. "Your new haircut looks great, honey. Very becoming."

Neal rolled her eyes and barely stopped herself from asking, *"Where's the pod, and what have you done with my real mother?"* Instead, she forced a smile in return. "You seem cheerful this morning."

"Well, it's a beautiful day."

"You remember I won't be home for supper, right?" Neal said. "I'm going straight from school to the . . . uh, the movies. With T. J. We'll grab a burger afterward."

"A burger? I thought you had become a vegetarian."

Neal felt herself flush. "Yeah, well, sometimes."

Her mother set the platter of pancakes on the table. "I remembered. As a matter of fact, I won't be here either."

Neal forked up two pancakes and poured syrup on them. "Got a date with *Chuck?*"

"Charles," her mother corrected archly. "As a matter of fact, I do. He's taking me to dinner, and then to the Flat Rock Playhouse." She turned to Granny Q. "Mama, I've made supper for you. All you have to do is take it out of the fridge and microwave the plate for three minutes. Don't forget to remove the aluminum foil." She peered into Granny Q's eyes. "You'll be all right without us here?"

"I'll be fine," Granny Q slurred. "Don't worry about me."

Neal looked across the table and saw a shadow pass over her grandmother's face—a haunted, empty expression. But she couldn't afford to think about that. She had to go or she'd be late meeting Mike. "Gotta run. Don't wait up."

"All right, sweetie. Have a good day." Her mother kissed her on the cheek and patted her arm. "I love you."

Caught off guard, Neal couldn't decide how to respond. It had been months since her mother called her *sweetie*, and she certainly hadn't said *I love you* in a very long time. At last she opted for the line of least resistance. "Love you, too," she said.

She paused in the doorway and turned. "And you too, Granny Q."

The old woman's eyes misted over. She raised a trembling hand and opened her mouth to speak.

But Neal couldn't wait. She grabbed her backpack off the chair and bolted for the door.

Edith watched as her granddaughter dashed from the room. Something was up with that child, and she was pretty sure she knew what it was. But she couldn't seem to make Abby listen long enough to get through to her.

"It's nice to see Neal Grace so happy these days," Abby said. "Maybe this family is finally getting back on track."

Edith shook her head. "I'm worried about her."

"Worried, did you say?" Abby stared at

her as if she'd lost her mind as well as her mobility. "There's nothing to worry about, Mama. The punky hair style and the clothes don't mean anything. Teenagers need to have their little rebellions. I'm just glad she's spending time with her friends and being— well, *normal* for a change." She sighed and gazed over Edith's head. "I know it's hard for you to understand, but I think Neal Grace is finally coming around."

Edith didn't answer. Instead, she struggled to cut off a bite of pancake. Her fork wasn't working properly, and the pancake slid off into her lap. Despite her best efforts, tears welled up in her eyes.

Abby didn't notice. She had already gotten up and was clearing the table, still talking. "You do like Charles, don't you, Mama? He's so—what's the word? Stable. Dependable. Just the kind of man I need in my life. He makes everything seem so much *simpler*. Oh, I'm not going to do anything silly like run off and get married. But I do enjoy his company, and—"

On she rambled, not waiting for a response. Edith sat there half-listening, glad for once that communication was so difficult for her. Her daughter wouldn't have wanted to hear what she had to say about Charles Bingham.

Abby finished loading the dishwasher and turned. "I'm off to work, Mama. You take care of yourself. I'll be home around midnight, I'd guess." She leaned over, kissed Edith on the cheek, and was gone.

And Edith sat there, alone at the kitchen table, her hand pressed to the kiss she could no longer feel.

The day seemed to grind by in slow motion. Abby wasn't getting anything accomplished. She sat at her desk, surrounded by proofs for the November issue of the magazine, concocting an elaborate daydream in which she married Charles Bingham, quit her job, and let him take on the responsibilities of making a living and worrying about the upstairs plumbing and making sure Mama and Neal Grace were properly cared for.

It was an attractive dream. But one question continued to plague her. Did she love Charles? Maybe—if love could be defined as mutual compatibility, or shared values, or complementary intellectual interests. She didn't have particularly passionate feelings for the man, but he was a good person with a solid, stable life. She could do worse.

And besides, the one person who *did* generate heat in Abby's soul was completely unsuitable as a candidate for a long-term relationship.

Abby thought about the last time she had been with Devin Connor. She had contrived a reason to visit—needing to check some details and get a few more candid photos for the layout—but in her heart she knew that her carefully planned professional "reason" was only a thinly veiled excuse. She was just about to turn around in the driveway and leave when he opened the door and came out onto the porch.

She had gotten out of the car and stood in the clearing, looking up toward the cabin. He made no move to come toward her, but simply stood there, waiting. Abby took a deep breath, and without warning that sense of freedom and lightness rushed into her—the very feeling she had experienced the first time she rode on the back of his Vespa.

She hadn't felt that way since—since

John Mac brought light and color and meaning to the world.

Staggered by the unbidden thought, Abby moved numbly toward the cabin, holding her briefcase up to her chest like a shield.

"I'm glad you're here," Devin said when she was settled at the kitchen table with the pages of her article spread out between them. "There's something I'd like to talk to you about."

"All right." Abby shuffled a stack of photographs and pretended to be looking for something.

"Abby, look at me."

She stopped fiddling with the pictures and looked up. His eyes, blue as the Carolina sky, smiled across at her, and in the back of her mind she could hear echoes of his music. A baffling combination of emotions assaulted her—she felt bewildered and terrified and captivated and glorious, all at the same time.

"I've been thinking," he went on.

She willed herself to speak. "About—?"

"About us." He ducked his head and poked at the ice in his glass with a forefinger. "I mean, this article is almost done, correct?"

"Yes."

"And when it's done—"

When it's done, I'll never see you again, Abby thought.

"When it's done," he repeated, "we won't be seeing each other again. At least we won't have any *reason* to see each other." He paused and waited. When she didn't respond, he plowed ahead. "I was thinking—that is, I was hoping—" He exhaled heavily. "I was hoping we might come up with a reason."

Abby kept silent.

"Such as having dinner together."

Again she said nothing.

"Like—well, like a date." He took a drink of his tea, then peered at her over the rim of his glass. "You could give me some encouragement here."

Abby summoned all her will power to glance up at him. He looked so fresh, so innocent, so—scared. *Say yes,* the voice inside her head demanded. "I . . . I don't know, Devin," she hedged. "I'm sort of—"

"Seeing someone?" His face fell. "Well, of course. Of course you are. You're intelligent and attractive and interesting and—" He ground to a halt. "OK. I, uh, I really feel foolish now. So let's just get this done, all right?" He turned his attention to the layout. "I'm sure whatever you come up with will be fine with me."

They finalized the details of the article, and Abby had driven away, back to her black-and-white life, back to Neal Grace and Mama and Charles Bingham. But no matter how fast she drove, she couldn't outrun the sense of loss.

Afterward she had gone over and over it again in her mind, all the reasons she could not afford to open her heart to Devin Connor. He was a destitute musician, for heaven's sake. An artist. An itinerant who lived off the generosity of others. A caretaker. Not to mention a complex, enigmatic man whose very presence aroused in her uncomfortable and unsettling thoughts about her own values and priorities.

She longed for life to be simpler, easier, less burdensome. And Devin Connor, for all the external simplicity of his life, was complication incarnate.

Well, it didn't matter. The interviews were done, and the article was almost finished.

She had plenty of material and enough photographs. She would never have to face Devin Connor again. She could put him out of her mind and move on.

The telephone rang, and Ford buzzed her on the intercom. "Abby, call for you on line two."

She picked up the receiver. "Abby McDougall."

"Hello, beautiful."

At the sound of Charles Bingham's voice, Abby stifled a rush of disappointment. "Hi, Charles," she said with forced brightness.

"I'm just calling to double-check about tonight. Dinner at six? We'll need to be at the theater by quarter to eight."

"That's fine. Shall I meet you somewhere? I'll be coming straight from work."

"How about that new Courtyard place just off the Square? It's quiet, and I have something important I want to talk to you about."

Something important. Abby's stomach lurched. She closed her eyes and took in a deep breath. "Sure. That sounds wonderful. I'll meet you at six."

Charles hesitated, and Abby could hear him breathing through the telephone. "Is

everything all right?" he said. "You sound—
odd."

"I'm fine," she said. "Just busy, that's all.
I'll see you tonight."

With the lie still burning in her throat, she
hung up the phone.

10

When Wishes Come True

Riding up into the mountains on the back of Mike Damatto's motorcycle left Neal feeling chilled to the bone and slightly queasy. His friend's cabin was little more than a rustic shack with a broken-down fireplace and a hodgepodge of mildewy furniture that might have come from Goodwill. But it *was* secluded, and she had to admit the view from the rickety deck was pretty awesome.

While Mike gathered up a few sticks of wood to build a fire, Neal inspected the place. It was one small squarish room, with chinks between the logs wide enough to let daylight in. One L-shaped corner served as a kitchen, with a small rusted sink set into a scarred green Formica countertop. In the opposite corner sat a sagging double bed covered with a brown, hairy-looking blanket.

"Great place, huh?" Mike said in a breathless, heaving voice.

Neal turned. He was down on one knee, blowing into a damp and struggling fire. Smoke billowed into the cabin, adding more soot to the already blackened stones above the mantelpiece.

She came over to inspect the fire. "Do you have the flue open?"

"Yeah. I think so." He fiddled with the damper lever, and with a sickening metallic clunk, something black and heavy fell into the firebox. Sparks flew, and ash drifted out onto the dirty rug, but the flames caught and the smoke whooshed up the chimney. "Guess it's open now," Mike said with a laugh. He got up and wiped the soot from his hands onto the back of his jeans.

Neal sank onto the splintered wooden coffee table and stared into the fire. She was feeling rather green around the gills, and the smell of the smoke wasn't helping.

"You OK?" Mike asked, peering into her face. "You don't look so good."

"I'm just cold, and I got a little motion sick on that curvy road. The fire will help. I'll be fine."

"Got just what the doctor ordered," Mike

declared. He reached into his battered duffel bag and pulled out a six-pack. "Want one?"

Neal grimaced. "Beer? At ten in the morning? I don't think so."

"Whatever." He popped the top on one of the cans and took a long swig. "But I'm telling you, it's good for what ails you." Flopping down on the sofa, he stretched his legs out, propped his feet on the table, and patted the cushion next to him. "Come sit."

Neal complied. Mike put his arm around her and drew her close, and for a few minutes they sat in silence, watching the dance of the flames. Between the warmth of the fire on her face and the warmth of Mike's body at her side, she began to relax, and her eyes grew heavy.

"I been thinking," he said, his voice sounding fuzzy and far away. "You'll be graduating come spring."

"Right," she murmured.

"So there's nothing to stop us getting our own place."

The impact of his words didn't quite register. "What do you mean, our own place?"

He took a long drink of his beer and set the can on the floor at the side of the couch.

"Me and you, babe," he said. "Just the two of us. Together."

Neal forced her eyes open and sat up straighter. "Live together? Us?"

"Why not? You love me, don't you?" His jaw clenched in a hard line.

"Well, sure I do, Mike, but—"

"Then there's nothing else to discuss."

"There's lots to discuss!" Neal countered. "There's college, for one thing—"

He waved a hand to dismiss her objection. "You don't need college. I can take care of us. I make good money, you know." His voice carried a challenging edge, as if daring her to disagree.

"I know you do, Mike."

"I'm a good mechanic," he persisted. "Soon as I raise the cash, I'm gonna buy the shop."

"That's great, Mike, but—"

He lowered his feet to the floor with a thud and turned to face her. "But what? You don't want to be with me? I'm not good enough for you?"

"Of course you are," she soothed. "I'm here, aren't I? With you?"

"Yeah. But—" He narrowed his eyes and scanned her face, as if looking for something. "You been with somebody else? 'Cause if you have, I'll put him out of commission, I swear I will."

A familiar wrench of fear twisted in her stomach. "No, Mike. There's nobody else. Only you."

"But you don't want to live with me." He got up and paced across the room—three steps—then turned back to her, his fists clenched at his side. "I don't get it. You say you love me, you use me, and then when you're done with me—"

"I didn't say any of those things, Mike," Neal interrupted, trying to keep her voice calm. "I haven't used you. And I didn't say I don't want to live with you. I only said we need to discuss it."

"OK, let's discuss it," he said, still standing. "Are you my girl or not?"

"Your girl?" she repeated. "Well, yeah. Sure."

"And there's nobody else."

"Nobody."

"Then we should be together."

"We *are* together, Mike," Neal said. "But moving in together is a big step. It's a serious decision. And I guess I never thought about living with anyone until—" She stopped. She couldn't say it.

"Until what? Until you were *married?*" He uttered the word as if it were a curse, an obscenity.

Neal ducked her head. "Yes," she whispered. For all her talk about change, about liberation and independence and living the kind of life she chose, she realized in that moment that something in her still clung to the values she had grown up with. Marriage. Family. Purity of heart, faithfulness of soul. The legacy that had been passed down to her through nearly a hundred years. Try as she might, she could not escape it.

"Listen," Mike was saying. He had returned to the sofa and now sat close with his arm around her again. "I love you. I *need* you. Before you came along, I had nothing. No ambition, no future, nothing. You're my whole life. Without you, well, I don't know what would happen to me."

His words, clearly intended to win her over, had the opposite effect on Neal. Suddenly she felt overwhelmed, not only by her own losses, but by his expectations. Flattering as it might be to be the center of someone else's world, it was also a terrible burden, this realization that she must keep the universe in balance or another human being might go flying off course into destruction.

Mike was still talking. "We don't need to be married, babe. Don't you understand? What we got is bigger than that. We got each other. You wait and see. It'll be just the two of us—forever. I won't ever let you go. Never."

He was embracing her then, kissing her, stroking her face and shoulders with his grimy, soot-stained hands. He smelled of motor oil and beer. Neal's stomach turned over.

He took her hand, led her across the room, and pressed her down upon the brown hairy blanket. When she looked up into his eyes, she saw that lost-puppy expression, an earnestness that bordered on desperation. And she did not resist.

Just as she had not resisted before.

In an intimate, candlelit corner of the Courtyard Restaurant, Abby sat with her back pressed against the wall and her fingers entwined with Charles Bingham's across the spotless linen tablecloth. Night had fallen, and in the glass panes of the windows overlooking the square, candle flames reflected back like glimmering constellations.

Dinner had been perfect. Charles had ordered for her—a heavenly concoction of angel hair pasta with shrimp and scallops, and for dessert, a chocolate mousse pie light enough to float off the plate. Perfect. Until a strolling violinist stopped at their table. Then her mind spun out of control, and she found herself fighting back visions of Devin Connor's sky-blue eyes and easy smile, hearing in the chambers of her mind the music that gave wings to her soul and set her heart flying.

"Abby?"

She blinked and looked up. Charles was frowning at her, his eyes narrowed. "I'm sorry," she said. "I . . . I drifted."

"Well, drift back in my direction, will you?" He captured her fidgeting fingers and held them. With his free hand he reached into his pocket, drew out a small red box, and set it on the table between them.

"Charles, I—"

"Please, let me say this, Abby, and don't

interrupt. We haven't been dating very long, I realize, but we're not kids. We're two mature adults, and we know what we want out of life." He released her hand, picked up the box, and opened it. Inside was a modest diamond ring—not flashy or ostentatious, but very nice, very sensible. "What I want is you," he went on. "I want to marry you. Please say yes."

Abby stared, transfixed, at the solitaire. "I . . . I don't know, Charles," she stammered. "This is rather sudden."

He smiled at her, his hazel eyes catching the candlelight. "Fair enough. But before you come to a decision, at least give me a chance to make a case for myself. I may not be the most exciting man in the world, but I'll be a good husband to you. Although a college professor is far from rich, I make a good living, and you wouldn't have to continue to work unless you wanted to. I don't expect you to leave Quinn House, of course. I'm more than willing to live there. We're both sensible, down-to-earth people, Abby. We'd have a good life together; I'm sure of it."

"Yes," she whispered, "you're probably right."

She continued to look not at his face but at the ring. It made sense, really. Here was someone to share the burdens of life, to relieve her of some of the overwhelming responsibility she had carried for so long. With John Mac, she had experienced her one true love, the fire and passion, the laughter and the tears. A woman couldn't expect that kind of relationship twice in a lifetime. So what if her heart didn't leap up and shout when Charles entered the room? He was a good man—a safe, stable, reliable man. Life with him would be peaceful, if not passionate. Simple. Uncomplicated. Exactly what she had wished for.

A fragment of Devin Connor's music flitted through her mind, but she pushed it away.

"I know you'll probably need some time to consider my proposal," Charles was saying. "And that's fine. I can wait as long as—"

"No."

"No, you won't marry me, or no, you don't need time to think?"

"No, I don't need time to think. Yes, Charles, I'll marry you."

He took the ring from the box and fumbled with it as he tried to slip it on her finger.

It was too small. It finally slid over the knuckle into place, but it pinched her flesh and she took in a quick breath.

"I'll take it tomorrow to get it sized," he offered apologetically.

"It's fine. I'll take care of it."

He slid his coffee cup aside and took her hand, running his thumb back and forth across the face of the diamond. Abby looked at her watch. "I suppose we'd better get going or we'll miss the play."

"Right." He signed the check, pocketed his credit card, and stood, extending a hand to help her up. "Thank you," he said.

"You're welcome," she said, laughing lightly.

It seemed a strange response, given the fact that a handsome, eligible man had just asked her to marry him, but for the life of her, Abby couldn't think of anything else to say. The overriding emotion that filled her at this moment was not joy, or excitement, or even anticipation.

It was relief.

~

The house was dark and quiet. Edith had put her supper in the oven at 350 degrees, just like her daughter had told her. Neal Grace wasn't home yet, and Abby probably wouldn't be back until after eleven.

She shuffled through the living room turning on a couple of lamps, but the exertion wore her out, and by the time she got across the room, she had to brace against the mantel to catch her breath.

She ought to be using her cane, Edith thought. Even in the house. But something in her resisted the idea. An image rose to her mind—a feeble, white-haired old crone, hunched over with osteoporosis and leaning hard on her walking stick. Was that what she looked like to others? To her own daughter? To Neal Grace?

A tear welled up in her left eye. She tried to blink it away, but it leaked out and dripped onto the mantel.

She hated this. No one should live long enough to become a burden to the people she loved. And she *was* a burden; Edith knew it without question, even though Abby never said so. That girl could never hide anything. The expressions on her face spoke volumes, and the particular one she wore all the time these days was a look of sheer exhaustion and utter frustration.

Edith understood and didn't fault Abby for her feelings. There was only one place to put any blame for this: squarely in the lap of God.

"Why didn't I die?" she whispered to the empty house. "Why did you make me stay? Why leave me here half-alive and good for nothing?"

No answer came. Just the quiet ticking of the clock and the creaking of the house as it settled in for the night.

Her eyes wandered to the bookshelf next to the fireplace, where Grandma Gracie's Wishing Jar sat cradled in its velvet-lined box. From childhood she had heard the legend of the phoenix, that magical, mythical bird who went to its fiery death singing its sweetest song. Edith shook her head. She had tried to go down singing, too. She would have welcomed death, embraced it as a long-awaited friend. But something—Someone—snatched her back.

With a shaking hand she reached out, took the jar from its place, and held it up to the light. "Why?" she repeated. "I wish I knew. I wish I could understand—"

A screaming wail pierced the silence, and for a minute Edith stood frozen in place.

Then she identified the sound: the smoke alarm! But that wasn't possible. Her dinner hadn't been in the oven more than fifteen minutes. Hadn't Abby said—

No, she remembered with a surge of panic. Abby had said to put it in the *microwave.*

The acrid scent of melted plastic assaulted her, mixed with the odor of burning cheese. She turned toward the kitchen, caught a glimpse of gray smoke wafting up toward the ceiling. With the Wishing Jar still clutched in her good hand, Edith ran for the door. She had to turn the oven off, had to clean up the mess before—

But she forgot. She couldn't run. Her left leg weighed her down like lead, caught on the edge of the living room rug. She was falling, falling . . .

The ginger jar slipped from her grasp and hit the rug an instant before Edith did. It fractured clean open and lay there, its two halves wobbling, the red-and-gold phoenix spreading its wings in preparation for flight.

From a great distance, she heard a heavy thud and knew it was her own body making contact with the floor. But she felt no pain. Her eyes were fixed on the Wishing Jar, broken, just out of her reach. Light seemed to stream from it—a pristine white light, glowing, illuminating everything. A light so bright she could see nothing else.

Her head swam with dizzying speed, and a flash like lightning caught her behind the eyes. But nothing mattered except the light. She had to reach it, had to get inside it.

If she could only get to the light, she would be safe and whole. And everything would be all right . . .

PART 2

What Was

Only a few fresh days are left to me,
while hundreds, thousands of used ones
lie behind.
I slide down the backside
of life's arc,
unable to reverse the gravity
that pulls me toward the darkness.
I could be facing west,
glorying in the colors of the setting sun,
and yet my heart cannot resist
the backward glance,
the longing ache,
the bittersweet nostalgia
of all the virgin moments
that can never be recalled.

11

A Glimpse of Yesterday

Edith couldn't tell if the light was fading or her eyes were adjusting to the brightness. She blinked, looked around, and sat up, leaning heavily against the sofa.

She was still on the floor in the living room of Quinn House. She was sure of it, and yet everything appeared so . . . different. The sofa at her back, for one thing. It was not the familiar beige couch she remembered, but a dark green velvet settee on curved mahogany legs, flanked by two matching chairs. Her fingers ran absently through the nap of the rug. It felt less matted and worn, and the colors were bright and vibrant. Everything seemed newer, in fact—the wallpaper, the woodwork, the Wishing Jar in its green-lined box on the second shelf next to the fireplace.

Wait. The Wishing Jar. It had broken

when she fell. Only there it was, in its accustomed place on the shelf. The red-and-
gold phoenix looked down at her with its
bright beady eye, and she could have sworn
it winked.

She heard voices from another room,
footsteps drawing closer. And then, with a
clarity that chilled her through, Edith realized she was not alone in the room.

Slowly she turned. In the corner, between
the sofa and the wall, a small child
crouched—a girl, perhaps three or four
years old, with dark blue eyes and amber-
colored ringlets framing a round, tear-
streaked face. She was wearing a blue satin
dress and black patent high-top boots.

Edith put out a hand toward the child, in-
tending to calm and comfort her. "Don't be
afraid," she whispered. "I won't hurt you."

But the girl never moved, never gave any
indication that she saw or heard Edith.

The footsteps grew closer. In the background, Edith now realized, she could hear
a low buzz of conversation coming from the
dining room. From her vantage point on the
floor, she saw a man's legs, swathed in
black trousers, come through the doorway,

followed by the lower half of a woman shrouded in long, full skirts of black silk.

"Abigail, darling—there you are!" the woman exclaimed. Edith's eyes traveled upward, past the cinched-in waist, up the high neckline to a face as familiar to her as her own.

Her grandmother, Gracie Quinn.

But not as Edith had known Gracie. This was not the venerable old woman with a countenance as soft and wrinkled as flannel. Not the grandmother with the beatific expression and heaps of gray curls piled on top of her head. This Gracie was young and vibrant, with shining auburn hair and flawless skin. Exactly like the portrait that hung on the wall in Quinn House.

Except for the smile. The smile wasn't there. The young woman's eyes, though not bracketed by crow's-feet, nevertheless held a look of exhaustion and unutterable sorrow. She was dressed all in black.

Gracie Quinn was in mourning.

"Come, sweetheart," she urged, kneeling down in front of the girl. "I know this is difficult for you, as it is for all of us. But you mustn't hide. Mama's here. And everything will be all right, you'll see." She sat on the sofa and cradled the child in her arms, giving no indication that she had seen Edith or even realized she was in the room.

Edith's mind spun. Was she dying? Or already dead? Rumor had it that when people died, their lives flashed before their eyes. But she had always assumed such belief to be a myth. And besides, this wasn't *her* life, and it wasn't flashing. It was going by in perfectly normal time. The only odd thing about the scene was that Edith herself seemed to be completely invisible.

A dream, then. Maybe it was a dream.

But dreams were usually made up of shards of experience, disconnected images, not whole scenes in such elaborate detail. If she were dreaming about Gracie Quinn, wouldn't her grandmother have been old, as Edith remembered her?

It was too much to figure out. Far too confusing.

"Are you all right now?" Gracie whispered, brushing a curl away from the girl's temple.

The child shook her head. "Mommy, am I going to die, too?"

Gracie took a firm hold on the little girl's shoulders and looked straight into her eyes.

"Abigail, you remember how sick your little brothers were?"

Abigail nodded.

"Neal and Richard caught a disease, an illness called measles. And they simply were not big enough or strong enough to fight it off. But *you* didn't get sick, did you?"

"No."

"We will miss them terribly, and we'll all feel sad, probably for a long time," Gracie went on gently. "But gradually the pain of losing them will get less and less, and we will remember the happy times. They will always be with us, because we loved them."

The child stared at her mother with wide, round eyes. "But I wished! On the Wishing Jar! I wished they would get well. Why didn't they, Mommy?"

Tears welled up in Gracie's eyes, and she pulled the little girl into a fierce embrace and held on tight. When she spoke again, her voice was strained and coarse. "I wished, too, darling. I prayed—we all did. But sometimes our wishes don't come true the way we hope, and our prayers—" She broke down and sobbed. "Sometimes we simply don't get what we want in life."

She released the child, accepted a handkerchief from the man who stood silent at her side, and dabbed at her face. "Go with Papa, now, and get something to eat. I'll be along in a moment."

The man held out his hand and ushered the little girl out of the room in the direction of the kitchen. Gracie leaned back on the settee, obviously trying to regain her composure.

Edith got up from the rug and sat in the chair at right angles to Gracie. She watched the woman's face for a moment, then whispered, "Grandma?"

Gracie didn't respond. But Edith knew. This *was* her grandmother, and if she remembered her dates correctly, the year had to be 1907. The year the tiny, premature twins, Neal and Richard, died at the age of eighteen months. That would make Abigail nearly four. And the man who had taken Abigail into the kitchen must be Kensington Quinn, called Kenzie—the grandfather she could barely remember.

Edith closed her eyes and tried to regain her equilibrium. The little girl was Abigail. Her own mother, for whom Abby had been named. The sole surviving child of Gracie and Kensington Quinn.

Edith knew about the boys dying from measles, of course. It was part of the Quinn family history. And she could empathize all too well with losing someone you loved— even after all these years, the memory of the death of her own two brothers brought pain. Not a devastating, debilitating grief, but a twinge of loss, a familiar bursitis of the soul that acted up when the weather changed. Her older brother—James Junior, called Jay—had been gunned down on the beach during the first wave of the assault on Normandy. Kenny, three years younger than Edith, had died in a military training accident before he ever got to Korea.

Edith had loved her brothers, and missed them still. To tell the truth, she had always secretly thought God a little unfair to take both of them. Yet the death of two young soldiers in wartime was infinitely easier to understand than this: twin babies, dead before their second birthday because they had come into life prematurely and were too small and weak to fight off a disease like measles.

Yes, she knew firsthand about the pain that came with being left behind. But hers was a sister's grief. She had never—thank

God—experienced the unspeakable horror of living through the death of her own child. Any mother would gladly give up her own life to save the life of her son or daughter. And Gracie, apparently, was no exception.

"God help me," Gracie was saying, "why didn't I die instead? And where will I find the courage to keep on living?"

For an instant Edith imagined her grandmother was talking to her, and she opened her mouth to respond. But someone else was the object of Gracie's plea. "They were barely more than infants, just two innocent little boys . . ." She clutched her fingers around the soggy handkerchief and pummeled the settee with her fist. "My darling babies."

Edith leaned forward to put a hand on Gracie's arm, but stopped just short of contact. She longed to comfort her, to tell her that everything was going to be all right. To let her know what a strong woman and wonderful mother her daughter, Abigail, had grown up to be. But it was just as well that Gracie could neither see nor hear her. Whatever consolations Edith might offer would be cold comfort, the pat answers of someone who had never suffered such misfortune and could not begin to understand her pain.

At last Gracie pulled herself together, rose from the sofa, and went to stand near the hearth. Edith followed. She hadn't seen, until now, the small walnut casket that sat on a bier to the left side of the fireplace.

Her heart twisted at the sight. In three-quarters of a century of living, Edith had never had occasion to attend the funeral of a child, never experienced such a brutal, gut-wrenching sense of finality. The incongruity overwhelmed her. This shouldn't happen. Children shouldn't die.

She peered into the casket, forcing herself to look, to take in the full horror of her grandmother's bereavement. The small waxen faces, serene in death. The doll-sized coffin, small enough for one pallbearer to carry alone. Two tiny bodies in one satin-lined box. Together in death, as they had been together in the womb.

She couldn't tell the boys apart. Identical twins, they both had light curly hair and cherubic faces, long feathery eyelashes that lay still against rosy cheeks. Only a few faint reddish pockmarks, evidence of the ravaging disease that had claimed their brief lives, distinguished one child from the other.

Edith's heart hammered, and tears clogged her throat. She thought of Neal Grace, that squirming bundle of energy who had calmed in her embrace moments after her birth. How could she have endured it if that beloved child had died before she had a chance to live? How would Gracie endure it now?

Gracie Neal Quinn, the first of a long line of "strong Quinn women." A citadel of courage and wisdom. A legend. Edith had grown up in the shelter of her grandmother's image, had believed that nothing could shake Grandma Gracie. By the time Edith remembered her, as an old woman, she had seemed perfectly grounded, at peace with herself, with God, in tune with the universe.

Edith had always envied Grandma Gracie's faith, had always aspired to be like her, had always fallen short. Now, for the first time, she began to realize that the inner fortitude and fearlessness that made up Gracie Quinn's character had been purchased at a very high price indeed.

Gracie leaned over the coffin that held her infant sons, and her tears fell onto their faces. "Lord, I believe," she whispered. "Help my unbelief."

12

One Small Touch

Reluctantly, Edith left Gracie to her grief. Gestures of sympathy would have been lost on her grandmother, and even if Gracie wasn't aware of Edith's presence, she felt like an intruder on the scene.

Avoiding the dining room where the mourners were gathered, Edith began wandering through the house. Except for the front parlor, where a fire had been lit, the rooms were cold and a bit damp. Through the window on the stair landing, her eye caught a slice of sky—not blue, but a gray-white bleakness. The sight disoriented her. She had no idea what day it was, what time of day, what season. That glimpse of gray might indicate winter, or it could simply be late afternoon, when the sky faded and began to darken.

Edith mounted the steps and stood on

the landing, peering intently out the window. Winter. It was definitely winter. Not a leaf remained on any tree in sight, and a chilly-looking drizzle fell steadily onto the street below.

Suddenly a realization surfaced in her mind—a thought far more disconcerting than the dismal rain that pattered against the window. *She had climbed the stairs.*

Edith raised her left hand and stared at it as if it belonged to someone else. She flexed her fingers, felt the tautness of the muscles that ran up her forearm. Age spots still freckled the back of her hand, but the hand *worked!* She lifted her left leg and set it down again. Did a little shuffling soft-shoe on the landing. Explored the left side of her face with her fingers.

There were no signs—none at all—of the effects of the stroke. She was herself again. A miracle.

Edith's breath came in short, shallow gasps, and she stood there until reason returned to her. Once, when she was very young, she had sneaked into a tent revival that featured a traveling evangelist and miracle worker. There she had seen an old woman kicking up the sawdust on the floor, dancing her praises and shouting that she'd been healed from arthritis or bursitis or phlebitis—Edith couldn't quite recall the details. She did remember, however, that all the so-called miraculous healings had been granted to people with invisible illnesses. No one got up from a wheelchair and walked. No blind eyes were opened.

Except, perhaps, Edith's own. As she had watched the spectacle, the scales fell away and she saw, for the first time, how people who were gullible enough—or desperate enough—could easily be conned in the name of Jesus. If you didn't get healed, the evangelist said, it was because you didn't have enough faith. If you went away sick, or if your crop failed, or if you lost your job or couldn't make ends meet, it was a sign of sin in your life, of something not right in your relationship with God. God didn't bless people who didn't believe.

The shouting and singing were still going strong when Edith slunk away and went home, pierced and bleeding from the sharp edges of her shattered illusions. Her mother and grandmother had taught her to believe in a God of love and compassion and grace, a God who embraced the lost and lonely, a

God who wept with those who suffered. A God who bore little resemblance to the vengeful, demanding Deity the miracle worker described.

But what if her mother and grandmother were wrong?

What if bad things *did* happen as punishment from God for insufficient faith, or the wrong kind of faith, or no faith at all? What did that say about Gracie losing her twin boys, or Edith's own brothers dying in war, or Sam's heart attack, or John Mac's accident, or her own debilitating stroke?

The thought of the stroke brought her back to her senses. There was no miracle. She wasn't healed. More likely, the disappearance of her paralysis meant that she was, indeed, dead—or close to it—and experiencing some kind of afterlife echo. Or maybe it was all just an elaborate dream. Either way, she couldn't control the outcome. Her life was over, and she would just have to wait and see what happened next.

She pushed away from the window sill and went on up the stairs. The upper level of the house seemed a bit warmer. At the top of the stairway, the door to Neal Grace's room stood ajar, and she peered in. A fourposter bed with a canopy dominated the center of the room, and the rug was scattered with half-dressed dolls and children's books. In the corner where Neal Grace kept her stereo sat an ornate Victorian dollhouse with tiny furnishings and little lace curtains. Abigail's room. But no sign of the little girl who would grow up to become Edith's mother.

A few steps farther down the hallway, she heard muffled sobs. The door to the master bedroom was half-open, and she slipped inside. Clothed in a dressing gown, her grandmother was lying facedown on the bed. Behind her, the window was open, and a warm breeze ruffled the curtains. A single bar of sunlight fell across the quilted counterpane. The illumination made Gracie's auburn hair shine like burnished copper.

In a far corner of Edith's mind, something unidentified began scratching around, scrabbling like a mouse trying to chew its way out of a shoebox. Then the truth broke through. Sunlight. Open window. Warm breeze. And Gracie here, half-dressed, when a few moments ago she was downstairs with the mourners.

Edith stared at the window. The upper

branches of an ornamental pear tree, in full bloom, waved in the wind just beyond the sill. She could hear birds singing. It was spring.

She advanced cautiously into the room. Gracie sighed, sat up, and swiped at her eyes, but gave no indication that she was aware of Edith's presence.

After a while Gracie rose, straightened the comforter, and went to sit at the writing desk next to the window. Edith followed, watching over her shoulder as she drew out pen and ink and a small leather-bound journal from the top right-hand drawer. She flipped through until she came to a blank sheet, pressed the book flat, and began to write.

19th of April, 1909
Today is the twins' third birthday.

Edith stared down at the page, and that sense of disorientation slammed through her once more. Third birthday? 1909? She did a quick mental calculation. The twins had died during the winter of 1907—mid-December, perhaps, she couldn't quite remember. How was it possible that sixteen months had passed in the time it took her to climb the stairs and enter the room?

Her mind reeled as she tried to regain her equilibrium. Then she remembered: either this was a dream or she was already well on her way to eternity. And neither dreams nor the afterlife conformed to conventional notions of space and time.

Gracie had continued with the journal entry.

Today is the twins' third birthday. It seems incomprehensible to me that my babies have been gone now nearly as long as they lived. Well-meaning friends keep telling me that the pain of losing them will subside, that time heals all wounds. Some have even had the audacity to suggest (as if it's any of their business) that Kenzie and I should try to have another child. A new baby to take the place of the ones who died.

Such logic represents the height of absurdity, and the most damaging sort of meddling. Clearly these Job's comforters have never lost a child, or they wouldn't be spouting such mindless nonsense. Besides, I don't <u>want</u> *another baby. I want back the ones God took from me!*

I suppose it might be considered heresy for me to even <u>think</u> such a thing, much less commit it to writing. But God—if there is a God—already knows what I think, so why shouldn't I voice it? Why shouldn't I tell God precisely how angry I am, and how my faith has been crushed and mangled by his apparent lack of concern? Where was God when my babies were dying? And where is God now, when my heart is broken beyond repair and my world seems to be falling apart?

Those final sentences struck in Edith's heart like a bell. How well she could identify with her grandmother's torment! She had felt exactly the same way when Sam had died, and again when they had buried John Mac, and a third time when she had awakened in the hospital and realized she was still alive. Abby and Neal Grace had assumed her anger and hostility to be a result of the stroke, a response to the paralysis, a frustration over her difficulty with mobility and communication. In fact, she had been angry with God—furious, enraged. Not because she was bereft of a full life, but because God didn't grant her the blessing of being completely dead.

Edith smiled wryly to herself. Perhaps her wish was finally coming true. Perhaps now she *was* dying, and soon would be free to pass through the curtain and join Sam on the other side.

She focused her attention once more on Gracie, who was still writing.

Ever since the twins' death, life has been less than futile. Simply getting through each day is a monumental challenge. Kenzie has taken over all responsibility for Abigail's care. I can't help wondering if she might be better off with no mother at all than with a mother like me.

Something must change, although I have no idea how to effect the necessary transformation. Time hasn't healed anything. My grief and anger have not gone away. If only I could find a way to hope again, to believe again. But God abandoned me when my babies died, and the faith I once had seems very foreign and far away.

Edith backed away and went to look out the window, marveling at the response this confession generated in her. All her life, Gracie Quinn had been held up as the epitome of the strong, unshakable matriarch of the family—the great woman of God, whose spiritual strength and faithfulness were both legend and legacy, the bedrock of Edith's own identity as a Quinn.

But Gracie hadn't been a supersaint at all. She had simply been an ordinary woman, trying to figure things out, trying to hold on to her faith in God when difficulties and struggles threatened to overwhelm her.

Just like Edith herself.

The Gracie she remembered from her childhood—that extraordinary, awe-inspiring, exceptional grandmother who loomed larger than life—had truly been a person of deep and unshakable faith. But apparently that faith had not always been unassailable.

A strange fragment of a verse flitted through her mind, something about removing those things that can be shaken so the unshakable things might remain. Had Grandma Gracie herself said that, or was it simply a description of the way life worked?

When the earthquakes come, Edith mused,

you find out what in your life is shakable, and what is unshakable. You discover the true foundations of your soul.

Grandma Gracie had been the bedrock of the family, the foundation upon which the Quinn legacy was built. But bedrock didn't just spring up overnight. It was formed through time, as the result of intense pressure.

Gracie's current earthquake had shaken her faith to its foundations. The pressure was building. And Edith found herself intensely curious to discover how her grandmother had found her way back to faith.

She drew near the writing desk and read the remainder of the journal entry.

If only I might be granted one touch, one word—just a single syllable of comfort or release from the God I once felt so near to me. A sign, just a small sign, that God still cares. That God understands my pain and suffers with me.

I have spent so long in darkness and silence. If God is not with me in this terrible tomb, I might as well end my life and be done with it. Kenzie would take care of Abigail. They would miss me, no

doubt, but their lives would go on, and at
least I would not be a burden to them . . .

As Edith read the words, the reality of
what Gracie was considering slammed into
her like a fist to the midsection. "No!" she
shouted out loud. "Grandma, no! Don't
even think about it. Your daughter needs
you! I need you!" She kept talking, pleading,
even though she knew Gracie couldn't hear
a word she said. "What would this family be
without you? You *will* get through this.
You've got to go on living—for all our
sakes."

She went to the door and called frantically for Kenzie, but of course he couldn't
hear her, either. Panic set in, and her knees
buckled under her. She had to do something, had to change Gracie's mind. Had to
convince her, somehow, that God loved her
and life was worth living.

"Dear God," Edith whispered. "Help her,
please."

Turning back into the bedroom, she
moved on shaking legs to her grandmother's side. Gracie was weeping now,
murmuring to herself. "Just one small sign.
One word. One touch. That's all I ask."

Tears pricked at Edith's eyelids, and she found herself joining her grandmother's prayer. "Just one touch, Lord. Just one small sign."

Without fully realizing what she was doing, Edith reached out and gently laid her left hand on Gracie's shoulder. The contact, so completely otherworldly, shocked her so thoroughly that she almost let go. Her grandmother's body under her fingers felt ethereal, incorporeal, a substance utterly unlike human flesh. It kept shifting and moving. Holding onto it was like trying to capture Jell-O, like attempting to halt molecules in their flight.

But still she held on. "I love you, Grandma," she murmured fiercely into Gracie's ear. "God loves you. Believe it. Trust. Stay with us, please." She watched as her own left hand, spotted with age but strong and sure, pressed down on the insubstantial flesh. Over and over she repeated the words. "I love you. I love you."

And then, without warning, Edith sensed another hand, more real than her own shifting grasp on Gracie's shoulder. A warmth, seeping through her gnarled fingers and down into her grandmother's flesh. It only lasted a moment, barely enough time to feel it. And when it was over, Edith wondered if it had really happened, or was only the product of her desperate longing.

Gradually, Gracie stopped weeping. She raised her head. She turned toward the window and looked out at the pear blossoms. She took a deep breath of the honeyed spring air.

And then she smiled.

"I feel it," she said quietly. "After all this time." Her voice was laced with wonder, and her eyes bright as she lifted her face to the sunlight streaming through the window. "Spring is here. You're here. Perhaps you were always here."

At last Edith removed her hand from her grandmother's shoulder and stepped aside as Gracie rose from the chair and went to lean on the window sill.

She plucked a branch from the pear tree, inhaled its fragrance, then went to the doorway and called for Kenzie and Abigail to come up and join her.

Edith, still shaken and trembling, slipped past her into the hall.

13

Looking for the Love

Edith sat in a chair in Neal Grace's room—
no, Abigail's room, she corrected herself—
and tried to sort out what had happened.
She had touched Gracie on the shoulder,
had said, "I love you." That was all. But in
that touch, and in those words, Gracie had
somehow sensed God's presence reaching
into her soul again. A sudden, unexpected
spring had returned to a heart caught in the
grip of winter.

How was it possible? Some pain-ridden,
cynical place in Edith's mind resisted,
protesting that neither she nor God had
anything to do with turning Gracie's life
around. She had merely snapped out of her
depression, found a way to pull herself up
and keep on going. A simple case of—

Of what? Bootstraps? Stiff upper lip?
Pure will power, guts, and determination?

No. This wasn't "a simple case" of anything that had to do with human effort. It
was a miracle. Or if not a miracle, then
something very nearly like one.

Edith fought to silence the scornful,
skeptical voice in her head—the voice that
had dominated her thinking ever since the
stroke. If she could just give herself over, for
one glorious moment, to the emotion . . .

When it came, it nearly took her breath
away. Joy. Pure, magnificent, pristine joy,
shimmering with clarity, unadulterated in its
simplicity, almost overwhelming in its
power. It swelled up within her, a golden,
flawless luminescence, pushing back all
dark and pessimistic thoughts and leaving
her filled with delight so strong and sweet it
threatened to make her weep.

More than well-being, more than happi-
ness, more than contentment. It was, rather,
an infusion of otherness, a sense of being
weightless, lifted up by an invisible cable,
connected to the soul of the universe, to the
meaning of life itself.

So this was what Gracie meant about experiencing the Presence, the touch of God.

She lay back in the chair and shut her
eyes. She couldn't comprehend what had

happened. But for a moment—for this moment—she would revel in the glory and try
not to ask too many unanswerable questions.

⁓

When Edith opened her eyes again, the light
had shifted. She knew she hadn't slept, and
yet she couldn't shake the sensation that
time had passed—minutes or hours or
days, she couldn't tell.

She sat up and looked around. Abigail's
room looked the same—or did it? Something felt different. Little things. Details. The
door was shut, and she could have sworn
she had left it ajar. The big Victorian dollhouse still sat in the corner, but it appeared
shabbier, more used. The doll furniture was
all in its proper place, and there were no
books or toys scattered across the carpet.
She couldn't quite identify the difference,
except that an odd impression kept pushing
to the front of her mind.

The room felt . . . older.

Edith listened. She heard no sounds—no
voices, no footsteps in the hall. She tiptoed
to the door, opened it, and—

Vertigo set in. Edith's head began to spin

as she took in the scene in front of her. Not the dimly lit upstairs hallway of Quinn House, as she had expected, but bright sunshine, so bright it made her squint. She was high up on a mountainside, and as her eyes adjusted to the light, she realized she was teetering on a rocky outcropping, looking down at the city spread out before her. She could see the Square and the Vance Monument and closer, off to the right, the road that wound up Town Mountain to the Grove Park Inn, and beyond.

Unless she missed her guess, she was standing on top of Beaucatcher Mountain.

Cautiously Edith backed away from the edge of the precipice. She heard voices, women's voices. She turned.

There, on a ledge to her left, sat Gracie Quinn. But not the old grandmother of her childhood memories, and not the grieving young mother she had encountered on the day of the twins' funeral. This was a handsome middle-aged Gracie, in her forties, perhaps. Her thick coppery hair, with a few threads of silver at the temples, caught and reflected back the sunlight. She was laughing.

Beside her sat a younger woman. Although she possessed that same rich auburn hair, hers was not piled in waves on her head, but cut in a bob that fell just below her ears. She wore navy sailor-style trousers and a middy blouse with a large square collar. Her head was down, and she was rummaging in a small picnic basket. When she'd found what she was looking for—a paring knife—she raised her head and faced Gracie.

Edith's breath caught in her chest as she recognized the face.

"Mother!" she cried.

No response. They went on laughing as Gracie took the knife and began to peel and slice a peach.

Edith drew nearer, her whole body trembling. Of course she had known, from the moment she entered this dream, that the child Abigail would grow up to be her mother. But she hadn't expected to see Mother like this, young and alive, so nearly like the woman who had given birth to her, raised her, taught her, healed with kisses the cuts and scrapes of life.

In an instant, seven decades fell away, and Edith lurched backward into her childself. She wanted nothing more than to run to her mother, nestle in her lap, feel her embrace, have her hair stroked and all her cares and worries loved away.

But of course it wouldn't happen. She could no more feel her mother's touch than Abigail could see or hear her now. She contented herself, instead, with sitting as close to the two as she could get.

"Isn't this marvelous?" Gracie was saying. "Such a beautiful day, and such an incredible view." She took a bite of the peach and handed a slice to her daughter.

Abigail gazed out over the vista. "I remember coming up here so many times when I was a little girl. This was your wishing place, Mama, your dreaming spot." She smiled. "Thank you for sharing it with me."

Gracie leaned back on her elbows and stared into the cloudless blue sky. "I claimed this place when I was a child," she said dreamily. "But my most vivid memory of being here came much later, after your father and I were married. It was the day I bought the Wishing Jar, the day my fondest wish came true." She sat up and touched Abigail's cheek. "The day I found out I was expecting you."

Abigail turned and looked into her

mother's eyes. "You loved being a mother, didn't you?"

Gracie chuckled. "Not past tense, sweetie. Once a mother, always a mother. But yes, I love being *your* mother." She sobered then and shook her head. "Being a parent is a rich and rewarding job, but it's also one of the most painful and challenging undertakings of one's life."

Edith watched Gracie's face, saw a shadow hover over her eyes. Apparently Abigail saw it, too.

"You're thinking about the boys, aren't you? I was so young when they died. I can't imagine how you got through it all in one piece."

Gracie bit her lip. "I'll not deceive you, honey, there was a time when I doubted I *would* get through it. I nearly lost faith in life itself."

Abigail scooted closer, closing the distance between them. "I need to talk to you about that, Mama. That's why I suggested we come up here today."

"About your brothers?"

"About the kind of woman you are," Abigail said. "You've endured the worst kind of heartache, and yet you still believe in

God's love. I want to be that kind of person, but I'm not sure I have the strength within me."

Gracie looked off into the distance. "You're nineteen years old, Abigail. I've watched you grow into a solid, sensible young woman. I'm very proud of you."

"I know, Mama. And I'm grateful. But that doesn't answer my question. Thanks to you and Papa, I've had very little grief and pain in my life. I haven't been tested. How do I know, when the difficulties come, that I'll be strong enough to endure them?"

Gracie turned to face her, and Edith leaned forward, eager to hear the answer. "You don't know. You can't. Until those times come, the times that afflict your soul and rack your heart to its limits, you cannot really comprehend the reserves of strength and courage that lie within you. But I will give you one small piece of advice. When your trials come—and they will come, sooner or later—don't look for the answers. Look for the love."

Abigail frowned. "I'm not sure I know what you mean."

"It's a great temptation, when grief knocks at your door, to ask *why*. Why did this happen to me? What have I done to deserve this? What must I do to fix it? Those questions, natural as they are, come from a misunderstanding of God, and of the way the world works. All of us suffer. It's part of being human. When bad things happen, we look for someone to blame—others, ourselves, even God.

"When the twins first contracted the measles," Gracie went on, "I prayed that God would save them, heal them. That didn't happen. They died. I wanted to know why, *demanded* to know. But there is no answer to that question—no good answer, anyway, no answer that satisfies. For more than a year I was so caught up in my grief and pain and questioning that I couldn't see anything else. I was hurt and angry—angry at God, for taking my babies."

"But you're not angry with God now," Abigail said. "You have a deeper faith than anyone I've ever known. What made the difference?"

Gracie shrugged. "It's hard to explain. All I can say is that I woke up. I stopped asking for answers and asked instead for a renewed sense of God's presence. And when it came, almost like a miracle, I realized, even in the midst of the pain and the loss and the anger, that God loved me. You loved me. Your father loved me. It was as if I were enveloped by love, embraced by generations of it—before me and even after me."

She paused and thought for a moment before continuing. "Remember the Wishing Jar? When you were little, you used to hold it up to the light, waiting for the phoenix to fly, hoping to get your wish."

"Yes, but I was just a child then," Abigail protested.

"Sometimes childish notions hang on after we're grown up. Sometimes we act as if God is a big, invisible genie who can wave a magic wand and make our wishes come true. Yet often we don't even know what we should be wishing for. We want answers, solutions to life's dilemmas, and in searching for them, we lose sight of the love and grace and mercy that surround us."

She smiled and patted Abigail's hand. "Look for the love, my dearest daughter. When life seems to go terribly wrong, when the storms come and night closes in, try to remember that the way out may not be *around* your struggles, but *through* them.

Take life as it comes, and look for the love. God may not always push back the darkness, but God is present in it."

The sun was beginning to set. Gracie and Abigail packed up the remains of their picnic and started down the mountain path toward home, with Edith trailing along behind.

14

A Prayer for the Future

Even without the paralysis in her left side, Edith had difficulty keeping pace with Gracie and Abigail as they made their way down Beaucatcher Mountain. They were accustomed to walking; she had the disadvantage of living in an era where people got in their cars and drove a quarter of a mile to retrieve fast-food dinners from a pick-up window.

As dusk closed in, she lost sight of them halfway down Charlotte Street. But there was no danger of Edith getting lost—she had lived in Asheville all her life and was only a few blocks from home. The streetlights came on, shedding dappled light and casting a romantic glow over the sidewalks, lawns, and houses along her way.

When she finally climbed the steps and

stood on the wide porch of Quinn House, the front door was shut and there was no sign of either Gracie or Abigail. Cautiously she turned the handle and entered the foyer.

Every light in the house was on. She heard voices and heavy footsteps overhead.

And then a scream.

Edith bolted up the stairway and paused on the landing, flattening herself against the wall as a tall, rangy man flew past her down the stairs. He stopped for just a moment and turned back, and she saw his face—young, clean-shaven, and attractive. Vaguely familiar. And terrified.

"Don't panic, darling!" he yelled up the stairs. "I'll be back with the doctor as soon as I can!"

Then he vanished into the gathering night, slamming the door behind him.

Edith heard a car engine sputter to life. She peered out the landing window to see a Model T roadster backing out of the driveway. It rattled off into the darkness, and she climbed the rest of the stairs to the second floor.

Another scream—coming, she thought,

from the master bedroom. She hurried forward, apprehension clutching at her throat.

The bedroom door was shut. A small
tow-headed child—a boy, dressed in
woolen knickers and a blue cotton shirt—
stood at the door banging his little fists on
the panels. "Mommy! Mommy!" he shouted.
When no one came, he sagged against the
door, slid to a sitting position in the hallway,
and began to sob.

Edith sat down next to him and leaned
against the wall. She wished she could take
him in her arms, comfort him, tell him everything was going to be all right. But he
couldn't see or hear her. And besides, she
couldn't very well reassure him when she
had no idea what was going on.

At last the door opened, and Gracie
emerged, looking tired and haggard. She
seemed to have aged several years in the
past hour—her hair showing more silver, the
lines around her eyes and mouth more pro-
nounced. She knelt down and scooped the
little boy into her embrace.

"It's all right, Jay-Jay," she soothed.
"Your mommy's going to be just fine. Come
on. Gramma will take you downstairs and

we'll get some milk and a cookie—how about that?"

Edith stared, disbelieving, at the two of them. Jay-Jay. Her brother, born in 1924. The eldest child of James and Abigail Nelson, who died on D-day, just three days shy of his twentieth birthday. How old was he? Three, maybe? That would make this year 1927, and if the sounds emanating from the bedroom were any indication, someone was in labor.

Edith's heart palpitated as the truth settled in on her. That someone was Abigail. Her mother. About to deliver her second child . . .

A daughter, who would be given the name Edith Quinn Nelson.

Somehow, on the trip down Beaucatcher Mountain and back home again, Edith had skipped four years. Abigail was married and already the mother of one child. And the frantic man on the stairs was—

Of course. *Daddy.*

Edith shook her head and tried to clear her mind. She felt as if she had landed in the middle of surrealistic painting—one particular painting, in fact. Salvador Dali's *The Persistence of Memory.* Time was incomprehensibly skewed, with clocks melting all over her inner landscape. If she were, in fact, dying, teetering on the border between this life and the next, then everything she had experienced so far was simply a preview, and the main feature of her own life was about to begin.

~

Jay-Jay had been put to bed. James, Abigail's husband, had been banished to the lower reaches of the house to pace and wait.

The contractions were coming faster now. Exhausted and sweaty, Abigail leaned back against the pillows and gripped Gracie's hand, taking advantage of a brief moment of respite. The doctor, who had arrived an hour earlier, crouched on an ottoman at the foot of the bed. "We're close now—very close."

Edith had been through this experience before—once when she gave birth to Abby and a second time, vicariously, when Neal Grace was born. She understood what her own mother was enduring. But Abby's birth had taken place in a hospital, and drugs had assuaged much of the pain. With every contraction, every scream, her own body writhed in torment as well. Children never knew what agonies they inflicted on parents, she mused. And birth was only the beginning.

Another contraction hit, and the doctor braced himself. "This is it, Abigail. When the next one comes, push. Push hard!"

Abigail took a deep breath. Edith leaned close, and even though she knew Abigail couldn't feel it, she laid a hand on her mother's arm. "I'm sorry, Mother," she whispered into Abigail's ear. "Sorry to put you through all this."

"My child, my darling child," Abigail breathed. "It will be worth it—worth it all—to have you."

Stunned, Edith stumbled back away from her mother's bedside. Was it possible that her mother had heard?

Gracie leaned over Abigail and held on to her hand. "What did you say, honey?"

"Never mind what she said!" the doctor snapped. "Push, Abigail. Now!"

Abigail pushed. A howl of pain tore from her throat as the infant, bloody and wet and wriggling, slid from her body into the waiting hands of the physician. "It's a girl," he announced. "A strong, healthy baby girl."

With an efficiency born of experience, he wiped the baby's face and straggly limbs, smacked her hard to get her breathing, and placed her gently into her mother's arms.

Abigail gazed down at the wailing infant. Tears welled up in her eyes and spilled down her cheeks. "Look at her, Mama! She's beautiful."

Edith drew forward, marveling. The puckered little face, beet-red. The thrashing hands and legs, so tiny, so perfectly formed, even down to the minuscule fingernails and toenails. A new life, with her future spread out before her like an unpainted canvas. Infinite possibilities in that tiny soul. And even though Edith knew firsthand what that infant's future held—its joys and pains, its struggles and victories, its mixture of darkness and light—she couldn't stop herself from thinking that this moment was nothing short of a miracle.

She leaned in for a closer look. The baby's eyes opened and locked onto Edith's gaze. Impossible, Edith knew. And yet it happened. Those enormous blue eyes—

wise eyes, old eyes—looked at her and peered straight into her soul.

〜

Once the child arrived, Gracie's exhaustion immediately transformed itself into energy. She changed the linens, dressed Abigail in a fresh gown, brought a new, hand-embroidered blanket to wrap the baby in. When all was in order to her satisfaction, she opened the door and called down the stairs.

"James! Come up and see your baby girl!"

Edith heard her father take the steps two at a time with a bouncing, eager gait. He burst into the room and went straight to Abigail's side. "Are you all right, darling?"

"I'm fine," she murmured. "Just tired." She pulled the blanket away from the tiny, wrinkled face. "Meet your new daughter."

James Nelson gently reached out to stroke his daughter's downy head. The baby's hand flailed out, grabbed his forefinger, and held on. A light came on in his face—an expression of complete enchantment and utter tenderness. "Well," he whispered, "how's my little beauty?"

Tears sprang to Edith's eyes. She

couldn't hold them back. She had always idolized her father, but when she was a girl, he invariably spent more time with her brothers—taking them to ball games, working in the wood shop, fixing things. And after Jay's death at Normandy, all the life seemed to drain out of him. She never doubted that he cared for her, but at this moment, for the first time, she understood how deep his love went.

He leaned down and kissed Abigail. "I'll go get our son. He should meet his new baby sister."

In a minute or two he returned with Jay-Jay, half-asleep and a little grumpy, dragging his teddy bear by the ear. The boy rubbed his eyes and squinted at the squirming bundle in his mother's arms.

"Here's our new baby," James said.

"Where'd it come from?" Jay-Jay demanded.

James and Abigail exchanged a wry glance. James chuckled. "From our love, Son—just the way you did."

"What's his name?"

"It's not a he. It's a she. A girl. A sister for you. Her name is Edith Quinn Nelson."

Jay-Jay threw his bear on the floor and

twisted his face into a grimace. "A girl? A sister? Don't want a sister. Can we send it back and get a brother?"

James laughed. "No, Son, we can't send her back. But you'll like her. She's pretty small right now, but she'll grow up and be lots of fun."

"Can I touch her?"

"Yes, but very gently." James lifted the lad and settled him on the bed next to his mother.

The boy extended one finger, gingerly touched the baby's hand, then pulled back as if he'd been burned.

"It's all right," his dad assured him.

He reached out again. This time, the infant grabbed his finger, just as she had done with James a few minutes before. "Whoa!" Jay-Jay breathed, awe-struck. "She's real!"

"Yes, honey," said Abigail, stroking his hair with her free hand. "She's very real."

"OK." He scrambled off the bed and retrieved his bear. "I guess we can keep her. If I go back to bed now, will she be big enough to play with when I wake up?"

"Not quite," his dad said. "But soon.

Before you know it, she'll be nearly as big as you."

Jay-Jay, ambling to the doorway, turned back and cast his father a look of utter disdain. "No *girl* will ever be as big as me," he said. Then he shuffled off down the hall, yawning as he went.

⌐

When Jay-Jay was safely tucked in again, Gracie returned to the master bedroom and stood admiring her granddaughter. Edith had seen that look before, that expression of love—had seen it every time her grandmother looked at her, right up until the day she died. Her grandfather, Kenzie, leaner than before, his hair now peppered with gray, stood beside Gracie with an arm around her waist. On the other side of the bed, James sat next to his wife, embracing both her and the baby. He couldn't take his eyes off the infant's face.

"We need to let Abigail and the baby rest," Gracie said. "But before we go, let me hold my granddaughter for a moment."

Abigail nodded and handed the baby over to her mother. Gracie cuddled the sleeping child to her breast and looked down into her face. Silence enveloped the room, a silence so profound and deep that Edith could almost hear the infant's heart beating in time with her own.

"Darling Edith, you are one of God's good gifts," Gracie said quietly. "Live fully and love freely. May you grow into a wise and compassionate woman, and develop a pure heart and a faithful soul. And when life becomes difficult and her way dark—" She glanced over at her daughter, who was smiling through her tears.

"May you look for the love, and not for the answers," Abigail finished.

Gracie nodded. "Be strong in the grace of God, secure in God's love, and in the love of this family. Amen."

Gracie returned Edith to her mother's arms, then she and Kenzie drifted off to sleep in another room. James stretched out in the chaise lounge beside the bed and pulled an afghan over his legs. "I love you, darling," he said. "Both of you."

"We love you, too," Abigail responded sleepily.

Then he turned out the light.

In the darkness Edith groped her way out into the hall and sat down with her back against the door. But she did not sleep. She had too much to think about, and a watch to keep.

A vigil for her own infant self, who slumbered peacefully in her mother's arms.

15

Connections

Edith had never experienced anything quite so strange. She felt oddly as if she had become her own mother. And, as mothers often complain when their offspring's childhood seems too short, time was speeding up.

But for Edith the acceleration was real, not imagined. The child Edith spent as much time at Quinn House as she did in her own home, and every time Edith turned a corner she saw herself, growing up at a phenomenal rate. She saw her red and wrinkled infant self morph into a round-faced cherub, watched herself take her first faltering steps and fall face-first on the living room rug, heard herself utter her first word.

The rapid movement of time tended to be unsettling for Edith. One moment she stood in the kitchen, watching as her toddler alter

ego got her first taste of strained spinach—
and finally recognized the source of that familiar stain that would never come out of
the woodwork. But a few minutes later, she
followed Grandma Gracie upstairs to put little Edith down for a nap, and when she entered the room, a child of five or six was sitting on the floor, playing with the big
Victorian dollhouse that had belonged to
Abigail when she was a girl.

Gracie was nowhere in sight.

The child turned. "Hello," she said.

Edith's knees buckled under her, and she
sank down onto the floor next to the bed.

"Are you all right?" the child asked. "You
look kind of pale."

"I'm . . . I'm fine," Edith managed. "You
can see me, hear me?"

The little girl shot her a curious look. "Of
course I can see you." Abandoning the doll
furniture, she went over to where Edith sat,
offered a little curtsy, and held out her hand.
"My name is Edith Quinn Nelson," she said
politely. "Are you a friend of my grandmother's?"

Edith shook her hand. The experience
was much like touching Gracie that one
time—a feeling of grasping something not

quite alive, not quite of this world. She pulled back and suppressed a shiver. "My name is Edith as well," she said. "What makes you think I'm a friend of Gracie's?"

"Because you're old." The child plopped down in front of the dollhouse again. "I like old people. They don't mind playing." She looked over her shoulder and smiled. "Would you like to play dolls with me?"

Edith scooted closer. "This is a very nice dollhouse."

"It belonged to my mother, a long time ago when she was little. Grandma Gracie keeps it here for me to play with when I come to visit. This was my mother's room, you know."

Edith smiled. "Yes, I know."

"I suppose you would," the child said, tilting her head. "You've been here a very long time, haven't you? I remember seeing you when I was just a baby." She handed Edith a tiny dresser and a matching spindle bed. "Those go in the bedroom, here." She pointed. "Since our names are the same, I'll be Little Edith and you'll be Big Edith, all right?"

"I suppose that would work." Her mind reeling, Edith placed the furniture in the wrong room and had to do it over again. Some long-buried memory scratched away at her subconscious. "You've seen me around here often?" she asked cautiously.

"Oh, yes."

"But no one else seems to know I'm here."

"I've told them about you," the little girl said. "But they don't believe me. They call you my imaginary friend." She frowned. "It's very annoying not to be believed."

The memory burst through. Edith's imaginary friend. Her parents and grandparents had shrugged it off, humored her. She had heard them whispering about it behind her back. It was because she was the middle child, they said, the only girl—

A lumbering sound, like a herd of stampeding buffalo, interrupted Edith's thoughts.

"Here comes trouble," Little Edith warned. "It's Jay-Jay and Kenny."

The bedroom door slammed back on its hinges, and a blond tornado roared into the room, followed by a smaller funnel that looked to be its miniature. Jay, about eight or nine, and Ken, not more than three. Edith stared open-mouthed at the two boys as they flung themselves down on the rug and began wreaking havoc on the dollhouse.

"Leave us alone!" Little Edith demanded. "You're ruining everything!"

"Us?" Jay sneered at her. "What? You've got your invisible friend here?" He got up and began tramping around the room, raising his knees as high as they would go. "I'll smash her! I'll stomp her!"

"Jay-Jay, quit it, or I'll tell Grandma Gracie!"

"Jay-Jay, quit it!" he aped in a singsong voice.

"Quit it! Quit it!" Kenny echoed, squealing with glee.

"Where is she? Under the bed? I'll get her!" Jay-Jay crawled on his stomach, reaching under the bed with both hands, but all he came up with was a handful of dust bunnies. "Here she is!" he exclaimed, sifting the dust down on top of the dollhouse.

Little Edith began to sob.

"Crybaby!" her big brother mocked. "You're just an old crybaby *girl.*"

"What's going on in here?"

Edith looked up, as did the children, and saw Gracie framed in the doorway with her hands planted on her hips. She was thinner, and her hair was mostly gray now, but she still made for a formidable adversary. The noise in the room ceased instantly.

"Grandma, he messed up our house," Little Edith accused.

"Is that true, Jay-Jay?"

"Yes'm." Jay ducked his head. "We didn't mean anything. We was just having some fun."

"We *were* just having some fun," Gracie corrected tersely. "Now, is that any way to treat your little sister?"

"No, ma'am. But she—"

"No buts, young man. Apologize to her this instant."

"Do I hafta?"

"Yes, you have to. Immediately."

Jay narrowed his eyes to slits and glared at Little Edith. "I'm sorry."

Edith suppressed a smile. He didn't sound sorry. Not a bit.

"Like you mean it," Gracie prompted.

"OK, OK. I'm sorry, Edith. I shouldn't have come in here and messed up your house."

Gracie raised an eyebrow. "That's better. Edith, do you accept his apology?"

"I guess so."

"Fine. Now, you two boys go outside and play, and—"

"But, Grandma," Jay interrupted, "Kenny's too little. He just follows me around, and he can't do anything right."

"Can so!" Kenny protested.

Edith saw the look of amusement that flitted through her grandmother's eyes, but Gracie managed not to laugh. "Fine. You can stay here and play dolls with your sister."

Little Edith's countenance took on an expression of shock and outrage, but before she could get a word out, Jay-Jay yelled, "Will not!"

"Then you boys can come down to the kitchen and help me fix lunch. But from now on, James Nelson Junior, I expect you to behave like a gentleman. Understood?"

"Yes, ma'am." Jay got to his feet, took his little brother's hand, and followed Grandma Gracie out into the hall and down the stairs.

Little Edith rolled her eyes. "Boys!" she muttered.

"They'll get better," Edith assured her.

"I doubt it."

"Trust me. They'll grow up, and you'll like

them someday. You'll be glad to have brothers. And you'll miss them terribly when they're gone."

The girl shook her head and put her nose in the air. "I can't for the life of me imagine."

Edith nearly laughed out loud. It was Grandma Gracie's phrase, with precisely the same intonation.

Little Edith stared at her. "What's so funny?"

"Nothing. It's just that for a moment there, you sounded like your grandmother."

"Daddy says I'm the spitting image of Grandma," she said, puckering up her brow in concentration as she replaced the doll furniture in the house. "But I don't know what that means. What does spitting have to do with anything?"

"It's not about spitting," the elder Edith said gently. "It means 'spirit and image,' I think. To be the spitting image of your grandmother means you are just like her, inside and out."

Little Edith pondered this concept. "I like that idea. When I grow up, I want to be exactly like Grandma Gracie."

You could do worse, Edith thought, *than*

becoming the spirit and image of Gracie Quinn.

~

Edith sat on the porch in the wicker chaise, alone, staring at the empty space where Sam's homemade swing would eventually hang. Through the trees she could see a bit of downtown and the mountains rising up in the distance beyond. The Blue Ridge—timeless and eternal, at once ageless and new. Caught, like Edith herself, in the nether world between life and afterlife, old as creation but fresh and young with each passing season.

It was the first time in her seventy-five years, Edith realized, that she had ever understood—truly *known*—the eternal nature of the human soul. This might be a dream, but it was real to her. These people were *alive,* as surely as when they had walked the halls of Quinn House clothed in bodies of flesh and blood. In real time, her time, they might be long dead, their earthly frames returned to dust. But their souls lived on—in her dreams, in memory, in the spirit that had been passed down as her legacy. Somewhere behind the curtain, they lived.

And if they lived—if the spirit truly did prevail after the body had died—then nothing on earth was more valuable than the human soul.

Grandma Gracie had tried to teach her that truth—not so much in words, but by the way she lived. Gracie valued people. She met them where they were and treated them with grace and compassion. She loved them, with all their faults and failings. She understood them. She motivated them to live with purity of heart and faithfulness of soul.

And she had passed on that legacy to her daughter, Abigail. Both Grandma Gracie and Edith's own mother had modeled the ways of faith. She had seen their trust in action countless times, had watched as they weathered all sorts of storms without faltering. When her brothers had been killed, Jay in 1944 and Ken six years later, Mother had been the rock of the family, and Grandma Gracie the foundation under the rock.

Edith's own child-self had said it: "I want to be just like Grandma Gracie." And she had tried with all her might to imitate Gracie's trust. She had adored and respected her grandmother, had set out to emulate her, but she always seemed to fall short. She had said the right words, gone through the motions. Still, when difficult times came—like Sam's death, John Mac's accident, the stroke—she had never been able to muster the faith to believe in God's continuing presence. She had always asked "Why?" and been angry when no response came. She had looked for the answers instead of looking for the love.

A dawning awareness crept into Edith's mind as she recalled that conversation with her six-year-old alter ego. All her life she had wanted to mirror the spirit and image of Grandma Gracie. But Grandma Gracie had longed to reflect the spirit and image of God.

Edith hadn't failed to live up to her grandmother's image because she had set her sights too high, but because she had aimed too *low*. She hadn't gone to the source. And as a result, she had developed nothing more than a faded imitation of a second-hand faith.

She was still pondering this revelation when the porch boards creaked and a shadow fell over her.

She looked up to see a small girl, silhouetted against the afternoon sunlight. Little Edith, coming to find her, wanting her to play, no doubt. She smiled and opened her mouth to speak.

But before she could get a word out, another figure stepped onto the porch. A man, who came to stand behind the child, putting his hands on her shoulders. His torso blocked out the sun, and she saw.

Edith's heart nearly stopped beating, and she gasped for breath. The little girl wasn't her child-self. It was Abby. Her own daughter.

And the man behind her was Sam.

16

Passing the Torch

His attitude somber, his brow knitted into an expression of concern, Sam approached Edith and held out a hand. She didn't move, didn't dare breathe for fear he would vanish like the early mist on the mountains.

Instead, she simply gazed at him, drinking in the sight of him. So young and handsome, with smooth, clear skin and those irresistible brown eyes. She could feel her heart melting as she looked into his face. The only man she had ever loved.

"Mama, are you all right?" the little girl asked, and in her words Edith heard an echo of the adult Abby asking her the very same question. "What are you doing sitting out here all alone?"

She blinked. Shut her eyes and opened them again. Sam was still there. And he was frowning at her.

He squeezed little Abby's shoulder. "Your mama needed some time alone, honey. Go on back in the house. We'll be there in a minute."

The child obeyed, and Sam came to sit near Edith on the foot of the chaise lounge. So close. She caught a whiff of him, the lingering scent of Old Spice and cherry pipe tobacco. His nearness set her adrift, made every nerve in her body vibrate with anticipation.

Perhaps her wish had finally come true. Perhaps she had died, and Sam had come to her at last.

But what about Abby? If Edith were dead and this was heaven, Abby shouldn't be here. No. Abby was very much alive. Unless—

"Sweetheart?"

His voice, low and entreating, interrupted her thoughts. As if in slow motion, she saw him lean toward her, reaching out . . .

Their fingers touched, and his hand closed over hers. Warm flesh, solid, human. Real.

"I . . . I don't understand—," she began.

"I know, darling. It's hard. But you need to come in now. She's asking for you."

Edith's mind balked for a moment, then stuttered into motion again. Abby at age six. Sam, young and dashing, only slightly older than the way she remembered him when they married. He must be—what? Thirty? Thirty-one?

The truth came rushing at her, terrifying in its intensity. She was twenty-nine. It was summer. Grandma Gracie was dying.

"No," she whispered. "It can't be. It's too soon. I need more time."

Sam shook his head. "There is no more time, I'm afraid. You know this was the way Gracie wanted it, darling—to die at home, with her family around her."

"Yes, but—" Edith couldn't go on. She began to weep, and Sam gathered her into his arms and held her while she sobbed against his chest. When her tears subsided, he handed her a clean handkerchief and waited while she wiped her eyes. Then he helped her up, put an arm around her waist, and led her into the house.

Until she entered the foyer, Edith had only vaguely wondered about the changes— why, after all this time of being impercepti- ble to those around her, she could suddenly be seen and heard and even touched, not only by her child alter ego, but by Sam and Abby as well. She had been too caught up in the joy of seeing her husband again, and in the remembered pain of her beloved grandmother's death. Now, as they passed through the foyer, she happened to glance into the mirror over the hall table, and her mind cleared.

Two images stared back at her. Sam, standing beside a young woman with puffy eyes and tear-stained cheeks. Herself, at twenty-nine.

Edith gazed into the mirror, pretending to blot up the remaining tears with Sam's handkerchief. She lifted her right hand to her right cheek. The reflection's left hand rose to swipe the handkerchief across the left side of the face.

She was no longer an outsider, standing back and observing the past from a vantage point of invisibility. She was in her own body. A younger, tighter, healthier body, to be sure, but definitely hers.

But how had she gotten here? What miracle could possibly have transformed her from an unseen observer to a—

She pushed the question aside. It was a

futile debate. Anything was possible in a dream . . . or in death.

~

As Edith entered Grandma Gracie's bedroom, ushered by Sam's firm grip on her elbow, a wave of remembrance rolled through her, an eerie sense of déjà vu. She had done this once already. She had endured the agony of her grandmother's passing and wished with all her heart that she didn't have to do it again.

But there was Grandma Gracie, nearly lost in the high fourposter, her skin sallow, her eyes closed and sunken. Abigail, looking exhausted and spent, slumped in the upholstered chair in the corner next to the bed. Edith moved forward to the bedside and gently took the withered hand in her own.

How easy it was to forget the ravages cancer had wrought in that body! Nearly fifty years had passed since Edith had first lived through this terrible moment, years that had softened the edges of the memory and dulled the ache. And the events of this dream—or whatever it was—had brought other images of Gracie to the fore, new visions of her youth and revitalized memories of her in middle age, times when she was alive and full of energy. Now Edith had to stand once more at her dying grandmother's bedside, relive her passing, and be left with a mental picture of Gracie weak and sick and all too ready to throw off this earthly cloak and meet her Maker.

Gracie opened her eyes and looked at Edith. "I love you," she whispered.

"I love you, too," Edith responded. Her eyes drifted to the writing desk next to the window, and her mind flashed to that moment of wonder when she had laid her hand on the shoulder of a young, devastated mother in mourning and whispered *I love you* over and over, until her soul heard the words and reached out toward life again.

From the look in Gracie's eyes, Edith wondered if she might be remembering the very same moment. The old woman held her gaze, as if trying to communicate some truth beyond the realm of words. Then she motioned for Edith to come closer.

Carefully, so as not to cause her grandmother pain, Edith sat on the edge of the bed and leaned forward. "I'm here, Gracie." She bit her lip, regretting the slip of the tongue. *Grandma.* She should have said *Grandma.*

A light of recognition flashed in Gracie's eyes. "Yes, you're here," she murmured. "Perhaps you've always been here . . . The jar," Gracie whispered. "Bring me the Wishing Jar."

Edith motioned to Sam, who left the room and returned a few minutes later with the little wooden box in his hands. He handed it over, and she opened the box, revealing the red-and-gold phoenix spreading its wings against a background of green velvet. She held up the open box so that Grandma Gracie could see the jar.

The old woman reached out and ran a palsied finger over the goldwork. She gave a faint smile. "It's all arranged," she said. "Your mother wants to keep the home she and your father shared while he was alive. So Quinn House will be yours—yours and Sam's and little Abby's."

"You're sure?" Edith shot a glance at her mother, who nodded wearily.

"Positive," Abigail said.

"Everything I have will pass to you," Gracie went on. "Including the Wishing Jar." She paused and fought for breath. The effort of speaking was taking its toll. "On one condition."

"Condition?" Edith frowned. "What condition?"

"That you remember the lessons of the jar. Purity of heart. Faithfulness of soul."

"Of course, but—"

"Don't interrupt," Gracie said, and for a moment Edith could almost see the old fire in her.

She smiled. "Sorry, Grandma."

"As I said, purity of heart and faithfulness of soul. Live so that when your time comes, you can go down singing. But as long as you live, *live*."

"She's rambling," Sam said under his breath.

But Edith knew better. Something shifted, somewhere deep in her soul. Her heart resonated with the words, and her whole being vibrated with the force. *As long as you live, live.*

"I understand, Grandma," she whispered.

"Yes," the old woman said. "Somehow I thought you would."

Then, with a smile lighting her face, she exhaled her last breath and slipped through the curtain to the other side.

17

Awakening

Dazed, and with her heart beating a heavy dirge, Edith kissed her grandmother's cheek, took the box containing the Wishing Jar, and stumbled downstairs to the front parlor. She replaced the jar in its accustomed spot on the second shelf to the right, the box open and standing on end. Just the way Grandma Gracie had always kept it.

Looking down, she saw that she still had Sam's handkerchief crumpled in her hand. She shook it out, folded it in half, and began to dust—first the jar and its box, then the shelf, then the surrounding shelves. She picked up newspapers scattered across the rug and stacked them neatly on top of the kindling box. Dusted the mantel. She had just moved to the bookcase on the other side when she heard Sam's voice behind her.

"Edith, stop."

"I can't," she managed to say around the lump in her throat. "Everything's so dirty. Grandma likes the house neat and orderly, you know. I have to—"

Sam's strong arms clamped around her from behind. "It'll wait, sweetheart."

"No, it won't wait!" In a rage she turned in his arms and began to pummel her fists against his chest. "I need her. Don't you understand? I need—"

She broke down then, sobbing against him, limp in his arms. He helped her across the room and eased her to a sitting position on the floor, with her back to the sofa. Then he sank down beside her and gathered her into his arms again.

"Let go," he whispered. "It's all right; I've got you."

For a long time she cried—hours, maybe. Days. Years. At first she wept for the loss of Grandma Gracie, and then gradually she began to mourn the other losses of her life. Her brothers, killed by the senseless violence of war. Her father, who simply gave up living less than a year after his second son had been buried. Her mother. Her husband who, even though he held her this very moment, was still lost to her. John Mac, her son-in-law, the son of her heart if not of her body.

And then, at last, she began to weep for herself. For the woman she had become after the stroke, for the lack of connection with her daughter. For the lost bond between herself and Neal Grace—a bereavement that was, perhaps, the worst of all.

She cried, and Sam held her. Held her and waited. Stroked her hair and murmured how much he loved her, and how he'd always be with her.

At last, her tears exhausted and all her energy drained, she blew her nose on the dusty handkerchief, sagged against him, and slept.

⌒

The images of the dream were jumbled and disconnected, but Edith knew instinctively what she was seeing. Her life, passing before her, just as people said it would at the moment of death.

The dollhouse. Her mother's Victorian dollhouse, with the back panel removed to expose all the rooms to view. As in a surrealistic film, her view zoomed in on one of the upstairs bedrooms. There was a poster bed, and an area rug on the old oak floorboards, and in the corner a miniature of the doll-house itself. In front of this smaller doll-house, a tiny girl doll had been placed, as if playing with the house, arranging the furniture. And in the corner of that miniature room, another miniature, and on and on, reduced to infinity.

Closer and closer she moved. With a start, Edith realized that this wasn't the doll-house at all—it was Quinn House. Abigail's room. Her own childhood sanctuary. Neal Grace's room.

And the doll in the corner was moving.

It was Abby. She turned and smiled and waved, then returned her attention to arranging the furniture.

The scene shifted and moved to the lower level of the house, focusing in on the door that led to the front porch. The door swung open to reveal Sam—a tiny Sam on a little ladder, struggling to hang the swing he had made for her. He looked up and grinned. The hook above his head gave way and the swing clattered to the porch floor. He laughed and shrugged, then went back to work.

Edith's dream took her from the porch and around the side of the house to the back garden. It was spring. Miniature pink dogwoods and little white pear trees were in full bloom. At the far end of the garden, under a white trellis laced with climbing roses, stood a doll-sized Abby and John Mac, posing for wedding pictures.

Above them, the entire house was open on both levels. She moved closer, focusing in on the downstairs bedroom—her own room now, since the stroke. Feeling like Gulliver among the Lilliputians, Edith bent down to look.

Abby, pale as death, with dark circles under her eyes, lay in the bed with a wicker bassinet at her side. Edith recognized the scene instantly. Abby had been released from the hospital after Neal Grace's birth, and the two of them had come to Quinn House to stay for a while so Edith could help with the baby's care during Abby's recovery.

She willed herself closer, focusing on the bassinet. The tiny infant smiled as her grandmother drew near, waving her arms and legs and clearly wanting to be picked up. She was so small, barely large enough to fill up Edith's palm. Edith reached toward the bassinet to touch her . . .

But it was no use. The dream swung her away, moving rapidly through the house. She paused for a moment at the fireplace in the parlor and focused on the tiny Wishing Jar in its accustomed place on the second shelf to the right. Then she veered out the door again, past the porch and into the front yard.

A toddler was there, playing in the sprinkler—Neal Grace, soaking wet, covered with mud, and squealing with glee. When she saw her grandmother, she ran toward her, holding up her chubby arms. Edith's heart leaped at the sight. Nothing mattered—not the water or the mud or the mess. Nothing except getting to the beloved child and holding her once more.

Before she could reach the little girl's side, however, the scene shifted again. In the dream Edith felt tears sting her eyes, but there was nothing she could do to stop the fast-forward movement of time. She shuddered with a chill and saw snowflakes beginning to sift from a pewter sky. Above her head she heard someone laughing, and looked up to see Sam, dressed as Santa Claus, wobbling unsteadily on the roof.

Then she was inside the house, where a lighted Christmas tree filled the open foyer and rose almost to the top of the stairway. In the dining room, everyone was gathered around a table. Sam was carving the turkey. John Mac sat at his side, serving up a mountainous helping of mashed potatoes to a protesting Abby, while Neal Grace had gone red in the face from giggling. Carols drifted through the house from an unseen stereo.

The music faded, the lights dimmed, and Edith found herself peering into the tiny parlor. Fifty or sixty people milled about, most of them dressed in black. They spoke in hushed tones of Sam, what a wonderful man he had been, and how he would be missed. A twelve-year-old Neal Grace, lost and awkward, hovered in a corner next to the fireplace, clutching the Wishing Jar in her hands.

Back in the dining room, Abby stood absently arranging and rearranging cookies on a plate. She wore a black knit dress and no jewelry, and her eyes appeared empty and haunted. Someone—Edith didn't know who—came up to her and hugged her, expressing sympathy for her loss. When the scene shifted to the parlor again, Neal was still in her corner, but now she was three years older, a teenager, and her face bore an expression of anger and despair.

"Wait!" Edith called out in her sleep, but there was no halting the acceleration of time. The heavy bass of rock music pounded down into the parlor from upstairs. The house darkened and expanded around her, growing from a dollhouse into a full-size two-story brick home. She heard a faint voice calling for help. Then she smelled something burning and turned toward the kitchen. But her foot caught on the rug, and she felt herself falling, falling . . .

Edith jerked awake, her heart hammering and her palms sweating. She was still on the floor in the parlor of Quinn House, still with her back up against the sofa, still with Sam's arms wrapped snugly around her. Her left leg had gone numb, and she couldn't seem to get it to move. She felt old and exhausted and incredibly heavy.

Sam lifted his head, opened his eyes, and smiled. "You snore."

"Sorry. I didn't mean to fall asleep. But I had the most incredible dream. I dreamed—"

"I know," he said. He bent down to kiss her.

Edith twisted to meet him, lifted her face to his, and raised her left hand to caress his face.

The hand wouldn't work.

Wrinkled and spotted with age, it hung there on the end of her wrist, pulled into a claw.

She looked down at her legs, at the varicose veins purple against the pale skin, at the shriveled appearance of her left calf.

She disentangled herself from Sam's embrace and with her right hand felt the left side of her face. The jaw sagged. The eye drooped. She couldn't feel the touch of her hand on her own skin.

On the rucked-up rug, just out of reach, lay the Wishing Jar, broken in half.

She turned to Sam and stared at him.

"Do you understand now?" he asked gently.

Edith's mind flashed through a series of

images. Gracie mourning the death of the twins, her mother on the mountain talking of dreams and wishes and faith, her own birth and growing up, Grandma Gracie's death, and those final words: *Live so that when your time comes, you can go down singing. But as long as you live,* live.

She sighed. "My time hasn't come yet, has it?"

He shook his head. "No."

"But what about—?"

"What about me?" When she nodded, he smiled. "I'm here because you asked."

Edith turned this cryptic answer over in her mind. What had she asked?

"You asked why," he responded. "Unfortunately, that is not a question that often gets an answer."

She gave him a grimacing half-smile, but couldn't think of anything else to say.

"When people ask why," he went on, "they aren't looking for an explanation, but for an affirmation. The promise that the world still holds meaning, that their lives are significant. That the presence is still with them, no matter how fierce the storm or how dark the night."

Pieces of the puzzle began to fall into

place. Gracie, devastated by the death of her boys, had demanded to know *why*. But what she really wanted was an assurance that God had not abandoned her in her hour of grief and anger. She wanted a glimpse of grace. A breath of spring. A small reminder that hope still prevailed.

When that hope came to her, she went on to live a life marked by faith, by trust in the One who would never abandon her. Her "Why?" had been replaced by a far more significant question: "Who?"

And to that, Gracie knew the answer.

Edith lifted her clawlike left hand and stared at it. This same hand, *her* hand, had rested on Gracie's shoulder, had clasped that unsubstantial flesh and held on. *Her* voice had whispered "I love you" in Gracie's ear. *Her* presence had drawn Gracie back from the brink of annihilation.

But suddenly, with a lucidity that left her breathless, Edith knew the truth.

It wasn't *her* presence that had been there with Gracie that day, any more than it was Sam's presence that comforted her now.

"You're here," she whispered, looking

into his eyes. "Perhaps you've always been here."

He kissed her sagging cheek, smiled, and stood to his feet. As she watched, he walked over to where the Wishing Jar lay broken on the rug, stooped down, and picked it up.

"Wishes are like prayers," he mused. "Some of them are answered in simple, uncomplicated ways. But others are far more complex than we can ever dream."

He extended the two halves of the Wishing Jar, one in each hand. The porcelain surfaces of the interior of the jar began to glow with that same white light Edith had seen before. It grew brighter and brighter until it seemed as if Sam's whole body radiated with the illumination. She squinted against the brilliance, but could barely see his face.

"Certain miracles," he whispered, "are clear as crystal, so obvious we cannot possibly miss them. But some are hidden and hard to find." He began to bring the two halves of the jar together, slowly, deliberately. The light increased, its intensity almost blinding.

"Your wait is almost over," he said, smiling at her through the splendor. "But until the time comes, *live*. Look for the love. It is all around you."

The jagged pieces of the Wishing Jar met at the seams, two fragmented halves joining to make a whole. The light vanished. Sam was gone. The jar dropped unbroken to the rug and rolled in a wobbly line toward Edith's outstretched hand.

She blinked and exhaled the breath she had been holding. And then she heard footsteps on the porch and the sound of a key turning in the lock.

PART 3

What Is, and Is To Come

The ridge is high,
the vista long.
Both east and west stretch out
before me.
I can see it all—
yesterday's dawn, tomorrow's dusk,
from the rising of the sun
to its setting,
from one broad curve of earth
to the far horizon.
And yet at my feet,
in the cleft of the rock,
my eyes linger on
one small, new-budded flower.

18

Decisions

Abby inserted her key in the door and looked down at the modest diamond ring that had been pinching her finger all evening. Leaving the key dangling in the lock, she wrenched off the ring, dropped it into the side pocket of her purse, and rubbed at the indentation it had left behind.

Her knuckle was swollen. From the moment she put the ring on—and throughout the thirty-minute drive to Flat Rock, the three hours of the play, and the half-hour drive back to Asheville again—she had been intensely aware of it, clamped around her finger like a vise, chafing her skin, its intrusive, annoying presence demanding her attention. Had Abby been the superstitious type, she would have seen it as an omen, a harbinger of irritations to come.

But she wasn't superstitious, and she

could ill afford to find fault with a man like Charles Bingham.

Birdie had been right. He *was* a nice guy. So what if his kisses didn't exactly generate fireworks? Such passion was for younger women—women who hadn't already spent their lifetime allotment of the universe's favor. With John Mac she'd had twenty years with a soul mate. Two decades of love and laughter and challenge and growth—the kind of relationship other women envy.

She had already had *perfect.* Who was she to complain about *nice?*

The house was quiet when she entered the foyer. Mama was probably already in bed asleep. She slung her coat onto the hall tree, hung her keys on the rack next to the door, and tiptoed into the living room.

She smelled the odor first—a charred, pungent scent. Her brain snapped into high alert. Then she saw the wrinkled rug, the Wishing Jar lying on its side. And a hand outstretched, reaching for the jar.

"Mama!" Abby ran to where her mother lay on her side, on the floor next to the sofa. Her eyes were open and Abby could see that she was breathing, but she had a strange expression on her face. She was staring toward the center of the room as if seeing something invisible to the rest of the world.

Abby flung herself onto the floor next to the sofa, grabbed the phone from the lamp table, and dialed 911. "I need an ambulance!" she shouted into the receiver.

"No ambulance," Mama muttered. "I'm fine."

"You're *fine?*" Abby parroted, incredulous. "Mama, what happened?"

The garbled voice on the other end of the line was asking questions. Abby gave the address, threw down the phone, and focused her attention on her mother.

"Fell," she slurred, sitting up slowly and shaking her head. "Tried to run to the kitchen—"

Fire! Abby's mind screamed. She lunged to her feet and bolted into the kitchen. The charred smell was more intense here, and the red oven light was on, but there was no fire. She opened the door. In the bottom, splattered across the electric heating element, lay a molten lump of plastic mixed with burned cheese and cremated pasta. Breathing a sigh of relief, she turned off the oven and went back to her mother's side.

Mama was now sitting upright with her back against the sofa, but Abby didn't dare move her for fear something might be broken. Then the reality of the situation struck full force, and a wave of guilt washed over her. "You put your dinner in the oven instead of the microwave," she deduced. "And when you smelled it burning, you tried to get to it and fell."

Mama nodded.

"And you've been lying here on the floor for"—she glanced at the clock on the mantel just as it began to chime midnight—"six hours? Maybe more?"

Mama nodded again. "But I'm all right. Really."

In the distance she could hear a siren drawing nearer, and lights began to flash through the window. "The paramedics are here."

Mama shook her head firmly. "No. I'm OK."

"We'll let them decide that, all right?"

Abby opened the front door for the ambulance team, and within minutes they had determined that Mama had no broken bones, had not suffered a heart attack or another stroke, and seemed to be in no immediate medical crisis. "Still, we'd like to take her in, just to make sure," the female EMT told Abby. "She might have experienced another mild neurological episode."

Abby leaned over the gurney and took her mother's hand. "We're going to the hospital, Mama, just to make sure you're all right." She looked up at the paramedic. "Can I ride with her?"

The woman nodded.

"Give me just a minute." She bent back over the stretcher. "I'm going to leave a note for Neal Grace, Mama. She'll meet us at the hospital."

While the paramedics loaded her mother into the ambulance, Abby grabbed her keys off the rack and went to the kitchen. Rummaging in a drawer, she came up with a notepaper and pen. *Granny Q taken to Mission Emergency Room,* she wrote. *Bring my car and meet us.* Mom. Leaving the note and the car keys on the kitchen table, she dashed out into the dark night without even bothering to lock the door.

⁓

By the time Mike killed the engine of his motorcycle half a block from Quinn House,

Neal's whole body was vibrating. She peered at her watch, its dial dimly illuminated by the streetlight above her head. Ten minutes to one.

She exhaled a pent-up breath through gritted teeth. She should have been home hours ago. Mom had probably called out the National Guard by now, and no doubt T. J. had gone through the third degree. She'd be grounded until she was twenty-one.

But it wasn't her fault, not really. She had told Mike she needed to get home, and he hadn't listened. Around eight o'clock they had left the cabin, and Neal had thought they would come straight here. Mike, however, had other plans—plans that included a tour of several sleazy bars, two grease-soaked burgers, a couple of pitchers of beer, and one interminable game of pool. She hadn't had any choice in the matter.

Neal shook her head. Yes, she did have a choice. She could have refused to go with him in the first place. She could have called Mom on the cell phone and asked to be picked up. She could have—

Well, it didn't matter now. What was done was done, and she'd just have to live with the consequences.

"I gotta go, Mike," she said as she slid off the seat. He grabbed at her, pulling her to him for a final kiss. His breath smelled like stale beer and week-old ashtrays. She pushed away.

"Hey, whatsa matter?" he protested. "Don'tcha wanta kiss me?"

"It's late," she said. "I've got to get home."

She turned her back on him and walked toward the house. Behind her, she heard him cursing, then the Harley roaring to life and speeding off down the street. She didn't look back.

Quiet settled over her, the welcome silence of solitude. No matter what this day cost her in the way of punishment, it would be worth the price for what she had learned—namely, that she never wanted to see Michael Damatto again as long as she lived.

She hadn't broken the news to him yet, and wasn't quite sure how she was going to do it. But one long day alone with him had convinced her. Being with Mike was like being handcuffed to a roller coaster, whipped up and down, around in circles, over and over again. His need, his possessiveness, his seething anger, his self-pity. If she had to listen one more time to his grandiose dreams or his pathetic speech about how she was his whole world, she thought she would throw up.

She was exhausted, both physically and emotionally. How could she ever have found him remotely interesting? How could she have been so stupid? How could—

Neal stopped short at the sidewalk in front of the house. The lights in the living room were on, which meant Mom was probably still up. Waiting for her, no doubt. She didn't want to face her mother—or anyone—at the moment. All she wanted to do was take a hot shower, rid herself of the last remnants of Michael Damatto, and go to bed. Alone.

Heaving a heavy sigh, she shouldered her backpack and began walking slowly toward the front porch. Her mind searched for credible excuses for the late hour and the smell of cigarettes and beer. Maybe she'd get lucky. Maybe Mom would be asleep and she could sneak in without having to face a confrontation.

If she did get by with this, she swore to herself, she would never, ever be so stupid again. She would go back to being her old self—trustworthy, reliable Neal Grace—and never complain about anything.

How much would it cost in dollars and pain, she wondered, to have a tattoo removed?

She fished for her key. When she went to insert it in the lock, the door pushed open under the slight pressure. Her heart began to pound rapidly, painfully.

Mom never left the door unlocked, not at this time of night.

Her imagination launched into overdrive. What should she do? Call the police? Go inside? What if some burglar—or a rapist or a murderer—was lurking inside the house? What if Mom or Granny Q was hurt—shot, stabbed, bleeding to death? What if—?

She pushed the door open a crack. Silence.

Forget about sneaking in. All she could think about was seeing her mother and her grandmother alive and safe and well. A hundred worst-case scenarios flooded into her brain, as if someone had lifted a spillway gate. What would life be like without her mother? She couldn't imagine. And her grandmother! She remembered with remorse how she had treated Granny Q since the stroke—avoiding her whenever possible, acting like, well, she didn't want to remember how she had acted.

Fear ran a cold finger across her neck. If something had happened to Granny Q, she'd never forgive herself.

"Mom? Granny Q?" she whispered. No answer.

She slipped through the foyer and into the living room, holding her breath. Nothing seemed out of place, except that the rug was bunched up and the Wishing Jar lay on its side in the middle of the floor.

"Mom? Granny Q?" she called again, louder this time. The only answer was the ticking of the clock on the mantel. The hands jumped. A click. And then—

BONG. The clock struck once, and Neal nearly jumped out of her skin.

She breathed deeply, trying to calm herself. Through the dining room she could see that the kitchen lights were on. Her nose caught a whiff of an odor—like something burning.

Dropping her backpack on the sofa, she made her way into the kitchen. Something had burned, but she couldn't determine what. Then she saw the hastily scrawled note on the counter, weighted down with her mother's car keys.

Granny Q. The emergency room. Mission Hospital.

"No," she muttered under her breath. She grabbed the keys and ran for the door.

"Please, God," she whispered as she slid behind the wheel and started the car. "Please, let her be alive."

⁓

Abby sat in the chair next to the hospital bed and watched her mother sleep. There wasn't anything really wrong with her, the doctors had said, other than the lingering effects of the stroke, but they wanted to keep her a day or two. "For observation," they said. Run a few tests, cover all the bases. Just in case.

Abby smiled to herself, thinking that Mama's cynical observation about physicians just might be correct. *Doctors practice medicine,* she used to say, *the way a five-year-old practices the piano. They never quite get it right, but that doesn't stop them from torturing everyone around them and expecting to be applauded for the effort.*

She looked at her watch. It was one-fifteen, and the hospital corridors had grown quiet. Where on earth was Neal Grace, and why hadn't she come? Shortly after they had arrived at the hospital, she had called T. J.'s house. T. J.'s father had answered the phone, obviously half-asleep and grumpy. No, he said, Neal wasn't there. As far as he knew, she hadn't been around for several days.

She had then called Birdie, who was a little more gracious about being awakened in the dead of night. Birdie hadn't heard from Neal Grace either. She offered to get dressed and come to the hospital, but Abby had declined.

Now she fidgeted in the chair, wishing for company. For someone—anyone—to talk to. If only—

A soft knock on the door startled her, and she jumped to her feet. "Neal?"

The door swung open noiselessly, and Charles Bingham's face appeared in the gap. He was still dressed in the suit he had worn for their date, his tie loosened and the neck of his shirt unbuttoned. "I came as soon as I heard."

Abby bit her lip. "Birdie called you."

"Yes." He entered the room a few steps, his polished loafers clicking on the linoleum floor.

Every click sounded like a gunshot to Abby's ears, and she glanced toward the bed, where Mama still slept. She put a finger to her lips. "Shh. She's sleeping."

He drew closer and reached out for her. "Is she all right?" he whispered.

"Yes. At least I think so. But they want to keep her here a couple of days."

"Let's go to the visitors' lounge," he suggested. "It'll be easier to talk out there."

Reluctantly, Abby left her mother's side and followed him down the hall to an open area across from the elevators, furnished with upholstered chairs, a small dinette table, and coin-operated snack and soft drink machines. He rummaged in his pocket for change, bought a diet soda, and offered it to her. She shook her head.

"Let's sit down, then." He pulled out a chair at the table, and when she was settled took the seat opposite her. "Tell me what happened."

Abby briefly sketched out what she knew of the events of the evening—the plastic plate of leftovers charred in the oven, Mama's attempt to get to the kitchen, the fall. "That's all I know," she finished, "except that she was lying there on the floor, alone, for hours. I feel so guilty." She tore a paper napkin into shreds and looked up at him. "Birdie called you, you said?"

"That's right." He ran his fingers around the top of the soda can. "When I got home, I phoned to tell them the good news, and—"

"Good news?" Abby stared at him.

"About our engagement."

"Oh. Of course." Abby had completely forgotten his proposal. She quickly thrust her hands under the table so he couldn't see that she wasn't wearing the ring.

"Anyway," he went on, oblivious to her discomfort, "after Birdie talked to you, she called me back. She thought, under the circumstances, that you'd want me here with you, to support you." He peered into her face. "She was right, wasn't she? You *do* want me here?"

"Of . . . of course," Abby lied. The truth was, Charles was the last person she would have thought of in a time of crisis. She wanted Neal Grace. She wanted John Mac. She wanted . . .

"Given the circumstances, I think we need to make some decisions," he was saying.

Abby frowned. "Decisions?"

"Yes. About what to do with your mother."

"Excuse me? What do you mean, what to do with her?"

"Well, Abby, if we're going to be married soon, we should be making these decisions together, don't you think? You can't go on like this. Obviously the best thing would be to admit her to a facility of some kind, some place where she can be properly cared for."

Abby blinked, not believing what she was hearing. "I care for her."

"Of course you do, darling. But you're not thinking clearly. You can't possibly watch her twenty-four hours a day. She's starting fires and falling. She could hurt herself badly, or burn the house down. You can't always be there to look after her. There are professionals who are trained to do this. It's their job."

She's my mother, Abby's mind protested. *It's my job.* "But once . . . once we're married," she stammered, "I can be there for her full-time. You said I didn't need to work unless I wanted to."

A curious expression passed over his features, and she saw the muscle in his jaw quiver. "Don't you see, sweetheart," he said, his voice oddly quiet. "Once we're married, we're going to need time together, just the two of us. Neal will be going away to college next year, and—"

"Wait." She held up a hand to stop him, to halt the forward movement of a conversation that was beginning to get away from her. "It sounds like you have this all planned. Put Mama in a home, ship Neal Grace off to college—"

"It's not like that." He smiled at her and captured her hand in his. "I'm only thinking of your best interests. *And* your mother's."

Abby jerked her hand away and stood up so quickly that she pushed the chair into the wall behind her. "I can't think about this right now."

"Of course not," he soothed. "I'm sorry. I probably shouldn't have brought it up when you're so overwrought." He rose, came around the table, and pulled her into his arms. "Tell you what. Let's just get your

mother well and out of here, and we'll discuss this later. And if you decide you want
to care for her at home, well"—he shrugged
lightly—"we'll just make the best of that,
too."

Abby's stomach was churning like a cement mixer, and her mind spinning at a
comparable rate. "OK. Look. Why don't you
just go on home and get some sleep? I'll be
fine. I'm sure Neal will be here any minute."

He pulled back and looked at her. "Are
you sure?"

"Positive. I appreciate your coming,
Charles, but I—well, I believe I'd really prefer to be alone when Neal Grace arrives."

"All right, then. Whatever you say." He
leaned down and kissed her on the cheek.
"Call me."

"I will." She stood there until the elevator
doors closed behind him, then sank down
at the table, put her face in her hands, and
began to weep.

~

When the elevator door opened, the sight
that met Neal's eyes caused her heart to
sink. Her mother, sitting in the visitors' waiting area. Alone. Crying.

She had come too late.

Granny Q was gone.

She took a step forward and let the doors slide shut at her back, expecting her mother to look up. But her mother didn't see her, and so she moved off to one side and waited, trying to compose herself, to get control of her own emotions.

Such a bizarre feeling, watching her mother like this, when she didn't know anyone else could see. Her eyes traveled over the hunched, rounded shoulders, the auburn hair, graying at the temples, the hint of crow's-feet at the edges of her eyes, the slight sagging at the jaw line. With a shock Neal realized that her mother looked . . . old. Old and worn out and in terrible pain.

Why hadn't she noticed it before? Why hadn't she been aware of the pressure her mother was under? She always seemed to handle everything so easily—effortlessly, almost. Even after her father's death and Granny Q's stroke, Neal hadn't thought twice about her mother's equilibrium; she had simply accepted—assumed—that Mom could pretty much handle anything.

Guilt and regret crested over Neal, a wave that threatened to drown her. She hadn't seen the toll life was taking on her mother.

Maybe she hadn't wanted to see. She had been too caught up in her own world—in the agony of losing her father and watching her grandmother suffer, in her stupid obsession with Mike Damatto, in her desire for change, any kind of change. She had been oblivious to everyone around her.

And what about Granny Q? Had she died without knowing how very much her only granddaughter loved her?

Tears stung at Neal's eyes, but she didn't make a move to wipe them away. All her life—from the moment of her birth, or so she'd been told—her grandmother had been there for her, had loved her and supported her and comforted her. But when Granny Q had needed love and support and comfort, Neal had bailed. Unable to bear the pain of seeing the effects the stroke had on her grandmother, she had closed the door and turned the lock on her heart, leaving Granny Q on the outside.

"I'm sorry," she whispered into the quietness of the hospital hallway. "Sorry for everything." But it was too late. Too late to make things right with Granny Q. She had run out of time.

Through a blur of tears she looked again at that devastated, lonely figure weeping in the visitor's lounge. She would regret forever all she had left unsaid with Granny Q. But she didn't have to make the same mistake with her mother.

"Mom?" she said quietly, stepping forward.

Her mother raised her head and squinted against the brightness of the fluorescent lights. "Neal Grace?"

In a flash Neal was at her mother's side, embracing her awkwardly over the dinette table. "I'm here, Mom. I'm just sorry it took me so long."

Her mother got to her feet and pulled Neal close, and Neal hung on for dear life, absorbing her mother's warmth.

"It's all right, honey," her mother murmured. "Everything's going to be just fine now." The sensation of her mother's arms around her brought back memories of childhood, when she would awaken in the night with bad dreams.

This was the worst nightmare of all. Only it wasn't a dream.

And with Granny Q gone, things would never be all right again.

~

It might not have been a miracle, but it felt like one. Like Easter morning, except that it wasn't Jesus coming out of the tomb. It was Granny Q.

Neal sat at her grandmother's bedside, watching her chest rise and fall. Mom had suggested that Neal go home and get some sleep, but she couldn't leave. She wasn't the least bit tired. When her mother finally managed to make her understand that Granny Q was very much alive, adrenaline had rushed into Neal's veins and energized her. She felt as if she could stay here for days, just watching, marveling, being thankful.

She had been preparing herself for a funeral, and what she got was a resurrection.

A song she had learned in Sunday school long ago came back to her, a song about turning mourning into dancing, about putting off the sackcloth and filling the soul with gladness. Neal couldn't remember all the words, but the tune kept bouncing around in her head. She wanted to leap and shout and sing and laugh. But this was a hospital, so all she could do was sit beside Granny Q and wait.

Another recollection surfaced in Neal's mind, a story that had become family legend when she was very small. Her mother had corrected her about some misbehavior—standing up in her chair at the dining room table, Neal thought. "Sit down," Mom had told her. She refused. After a second warning, and a third, she finally sat. But with the kind of rebellion only a four-year-old can muster, she said firmly, "I may be sitting down on the outside, but I'm still standing up on the inside."

Neal chuckled at the memory. She might be sitting down on the outside, but on the inside she was running around the room, shouting, "Thank you! Thank you! THANK YOU!"

"What's so funny?"

Neal looked up. Granny Q's eyes were open, and she was staring at Neal curiously.

Neal laughed. "Nothing. It's just so . . . wonderful."

"Wonderful?" her grandmother mumbled. "Not for me. I want to go home."

Neal lowered the safety bars on the side

of the bed and took Granny Q's hand. "The doctor says you can go home in a day or two, if all the tests come back normal."

"Where's Abby?"

"Gone to get some coffee, I think, and to stretch her legs."

"Sorry you have to be here," Granny Q slurred. "Sorry you have to see me like this."

Tears stung Neal's eyes, and she shook her head. "There's no place on earth I'd rather be at this moment," she whispered. "And no one I'd rather be with."

She squeezed her grandmother's hand— the left hand, the claw hand.

And the hand squeezed back.

19

Second Chances

Quinn House
Mid-October

The telephone rang just as Abby opened the dishwasher to load the breakfast dishes. She picked up to hear a gruff-sounding, unfamiliar male voice.

"Lemme speak to Neal."

"Just a minute." Abby went to the doorway and called through the dining room. "Neal Grace? Telephone for you."

Neal came out of her grandmother's first-floor bedroom and ran through the living room into the kitchen. "Who is it?"

"I don't know. Some guy."

Abby watched Neal's face as she picked up the receiver and slid up to sit on the counter. The girl looked apprehensive—almost frightened.

Abby bit her lip and forced herself not to ask what was going on. "I'll give you some privacy," she whispered and turned toward the door.

"Stay," Neal said, cupping a hand around the mouthpiece. "I won't be long."

Abby nodded and set about finishing the dishes, trying not to clatter the silverware too much while her daughter was talking.

"No," she heard Neal say. "I can't."

The voice on the other end responded. Abby couldn't hear the words, only a muffled, garbled sound, but she could see that Neal was disturbed.

"I told you, I *can't,*" she repeated. "I need to be home with my grandmother."

A pause.

"Look, Mike, I said no, and I mean no. I guess we probably do need to talk, but I can't do it right now. Not today, not this week. Maybe next week. Just chill. I'll call you, all right?"

She hung up the phone without saying good-bye. Abby hesitated, trying to decide whether this was one of those times when a mother ought to pry just a little bit.

"Everything OK?"

Neal picked at a cuticle on her thumb and

didn't make eye contact. Abby was just about to drop it when Neal looked up.

"I guess I need to tell you about this." She sighed.

Abby poured another cup of coffee and sat down at the kitchen table. "I'm listening."

"Well, see, there's this guy."

"Mike?"

"Yeah, Mike." She jumped off the counter and came to take a seat at the table. "He's—well, kinda older."

"I didn't think he sounded like a high-school senior." Abby peered into her daughter's face. "Honey, are you in trouble?"

Neal laughed—a tense, nervous sound. "Trouble? No, Mom, I'm not in trouble. I just—" She paused for a moment, and Abby waited. "It's like this. I dated this guy for a while."

Abby stared down into her coffee cup. Every maternal instinct within her screamed to know details. Where had she met him? When had all this happened? And why would her daughter go out with some older man—a rough-sounding character, if his voice was any indication—without telling her? But she kept quiet.

"Anyway, here's the deal," Neal went on after a minute. "I was having a pretty tough time, you know, with Dad being gone and Granny Q's stroke. Everything felt pretty cr—" she hesitated, and then finished—"crummy. Maybe I thought being with Mike would somehow make things better. Make me feel like I had a life of my own, you know?"

Abby nodded. "What made you change your mind?"

A strange expression came over Neal's face. Shame, Abby thought. Embarrassment.

"I guess I finally saw him for what he really was. I thought he was strong and independent. But he got so . . . obsessed with me. I felt smothered, like I couldn't breathe. And what a temper! He was jealous all the time, wanting me all to himself." She took a deep breath and met Abby's gaze. "But it's over. He doesn't know it yet, but he's history. And I'll never make that mistake again."

Abby didn't say anything for a long time. At last Neal broke the silence. "I guess you're pretty ticked at me, huh?"

"I wish you had confided in me earlier, I'll

admit," Abby said. "You're fairly grown up, but you're still my daughter, and I'm responsible for you. I want to meet the people you spend time with, to know what you're doing, and with whom. Does that sound overprotective?"

"Yeah, a little." Neal laughed. "But it's OK."

"You said this guy—Mike—had a temper," Abby went on. "Did he ever—hurt you?"

"You mean like hitting me?" Neal shook her head. "He yelled sometimes. But when I realized I was walking around on eggshells, afraid I'd set him off, I knew it was time to get out."

Abby reached over and patted her daughter's hand. "You're pretty smart for almost eighteen."

"I don't feel too smart," Neal admitted. "I feel like an idiot. I never should have gotten involved with him in the first place. He's been calling me every day. So far I've managed to put him off, but now that Granny Q's getting better, I guess I'll have to see him." She grimaced. "T. J. tried to warn me about him, but I wouldn't listen."

Abby grinned. "You can tell T. J. for me that she's pretty high on my list."

"Not likely. I'm already going to have to live with about a year of *I-told-you-sos.*"

"That's a small price to pay for getting out of a potentially dangerous relationship unscathed."

"Yeah, I guess so," Neal said. "Look, Mom, I know I haven't exactly been myself lately. But that's going to change. I promise."

"I believe you. Now, about Mike."

"Him again?" Neal contorted her face into a grimace.

"Yes, him again. When are you going to tell him it's over?"

"I don't know. Soon as I get up the nerve, I guess."

"Are you worried about how he'll react?"

Neal nodded. "A little. He'll blow a gasket, I'm sure."

"Then do it here," Abby suggested, "when I'm home. I won't interfere, but I want to be here just in case you need some backup."

"Might as well get this over with," Neal said. "You got any plans for Saturday afternoon?"

"If I do, I'll cancel them. I'll be here."

"OK. I'll ask him to come over. It'll be quick—at least I hope so. I want this guy out of my life—permanently."

~

Neal went back to her grandmother's room feeling immensely relieved.

"You look a hundred pounds lighter," Granny Q said. "What happened?"

"That was Mike on the phone." Neal shrugged. "I told Mom about him."

Granny Q gave her a twisted, lopsided smile. "Good girl."

"Yeah, I feel better. But it was hard to tell her." Neal slumped down in the chair beside her grandmother's bed. "How come it's so much easier to talk to you?"

Granny Q lifted one eyebrow. "Hadn't been, till recently."

"I know, I know." Neal rolled her eyes. "I'm sorry. I just—"

"It's OK. Everything's all right now."

"Yeah. But I still feel bad about the way I treated you."

Granny Q reached out and grasped Neal's hand. "That's all settled, kiddo. We're both on the right track now. Physical therapy's helping, but more important, my heart's better. And I've got you back. Nothing else matters."

"What matters to me is that you're still alive. I thought you were dead, Granny Q. I thought I'd never have a chance to make things right."

"Just goes to show," the old woman murmured, "we all need to live while we live."

"Well, you're doing great," Neal said. "You're talking so much better. And getting stronger every day." She grinned. "Squeeze my hand."

Granny Q laughed. "Already did my exercises. Go 'way. You're gonna be late for school."

"Humor me," Neal demanded. "Squeeze."

Granny Q reached out, grabbed Neal's hand, and squeezed hard. Neal feigned a grimace and fell out of the chair onto the floor, cradling her wrist. "Ohhh," she moaned. "I think it's broken!"

"What is going on in here?"

Neal looked up to see her mother standing in the doorway, frowning and trying to pretend she was angry with them for making so much noise. "You two are nothing but trouble," she declared. "I don't know what I'm going to do with you."

"Yeah?" Neal said. "Well, give us another week. Granny Q and I have big plans to go club hopping. She's going to wear my black miniskirt, and we're going to pick up guys and dance till they throw us out for being rowdy."

"That should take about ten seconds," Mom shot back. "If you want me to drop you at school, Neal, I'm pulling out of the driveway in exactly three minutes."

"OK. Let me get my stuff." Neal leaned down to give her grandmother a hug and a kiss. "I'll be home around quarter to four. Do your exercises!"

Granny Q contorted her face into a mocking scowl. "Nag, nag."

Neal grinned at her, then turned to her mother. "She's just impossible to work with." She headed out the door, but her mother caught her by the arm.

"What's this about a black miniskirt?"

"Oops." Neal glanced at her grand-mother. "Help."

"You're on your own, kid." Granny Q laughed.

"I'll tell you about it later," Neal said over

her shoulder as she made her escape. "Much later. Like when I'm forty."

~

When they were gone and the house had grown quiet, Edith lay back against the pillows and smiled. It had been two weeks since she was released from the hospital, and in that short time so much had changed.

She was beginning to get feeling back in her left arm and leg. Her speech, as her granddaughter had observed, was improving tremendously, and she didn't feel nearly so tired all the time. More significant than the physical advances, however, were the emotional and spiritual improvements that had taken place within all of them. Quinn House no longer seemed dark and oppressive. Laughter echoed off the walls. Family dinners were times of animated conversation. Everything felt . . . normal again.

She looked at the clock on the bedside table. Roberta, the physical therapist, would be arriving at ten. Ever since the hospitalization, Abby had brought her breakfast in bed, and insisted that she wait and let

Roberta help her bathe and dress. But Edith was fed up with being treated like an invalid.

Today Roberta was going to get a surprise. By the time she got here, Edith intended to be showered and dressed, with her bed made and a fresh pot of decaf ready in the kitchen.

She got up, shuffled to the window, and opened it as far as it would go. Autumn was in full color, the trees blazing with red and orange and yellow. Her downstairs bedroom overlooked the backyard, and she couldn't see much of the mountains. But the sky was a brilliant blue and the air brisk and full of promise.

She leaned on the window sill and watched as squirrels darted among the fallen leaves beneath the oak trees, gathering acorns for the winter. One of them caught a glimpse of her and stood on his hind feet, clutching a nut between his paws and chattering away as if she understood every word he said.

"Yes," she responded, smiling down at him. "Yes, winter can be difficult. But spring always comes again."

The squirrel skittered away, and Edith gazed off into the deep blue of the sky.

"Thank you, Grandma Gracie," she whispered. "Thank you, Sam."

She paused. "And most of all," she finished, "thank you, God."

20

The Uncharted Path

At ten o'clock on Saturday morning, Neal woke up in a cold sweat, a sense of foreboding looming over her soul like a black thundercloud. Mike was supposed to be here at two. She had to talk to him, had to get it over with once and for all. She couldn't stand another minute of this churning in the pit of her stomach.

But how would he react? What would he do? Neal knew from hard experience that he didn't take well to rejection. This past Wednesday when he called he had been all sweet and syrupy, telling her how much he needed her, and how his whole life and future depended upon her love. On Thursday he was surly and angry, accusing her of abandoning him. Yesterday he'd threatened to come over and take her away by force, to

get her out of the clutches of her "control-
ling, dominating family."

Every time she thought of him, a wave of
nausea rose up in her throat. What was she
doing, getting involved with someone like
him? How could she possibly have been so
stupid?

The answer came to her from an unexpected source—a line from a poem she had
read long ago: *All ports look like home to a
sinking ship.*

Everything at home had been falling
apart. With Daddy's death and Granny Q's
stroke, the torment was simply too much for
her heart to bear. She had nearly drowned in
it. Sinking fast, she had fled blindly away
from her pain, and taken shelter in the first
port that came along—Mike's love.

But what she'd found wasn't love. It had
never been love. Need, perhaps. Some un-
filled place in her soul. Maybe even a distorted compulsion to be Mike Damatto's
savior, to rescue him from himself.

Shame washed over her. She had done
the unimaginable—given herself without resistance to a person she didn't love and
wasn't committed to. And for what? One
short-lived moment of adventure and relief,

a brief and fleeting sensation of being embraced, cared for, surrounded by safety.

Well, at least she was finished with all that. By two-thirty this afternoon, Mike Damatto would be out of her life forever. She would have plenty of time to deal with remorse and guilt later. For now she simply had to steel herself to break it off with him and hope he didn't make a scene.

She sat up on the side of the bed. The churning in her stomach increased. The room swayed, and then began to spin.

Fighting against a gag reflex, she lurched to her feet and lunged toward the bathroom.

⁓

Abby had just come out of her bedroom when the bathroom door slammed. She paused and heard faint sounds of retching, and then the toilet flushing.

She knocked gently on the door. "Neal?"

The door opened a crack. Her daughter stood there, still in her pajamas, a sheen of sweat on her face. The odor of vomit drifted out into the hallway.

"Are you sick, honey?"

Neal wiped at her mouth with a wet

washrag. "I'm OK. Better now. Just a stomach virus, maybe."

Abby put a hand to Neal's forehead. "You don't have a fever." She looked at her watch. "I'm supposed to meet Birdie for brunch in half an hour, but I can cancel."

Neal shook her head. "No, don't do that. I'm all right. Really. Just—I don't know, maybe I ate something that didn't agree with me."

"Or maybe you're nervous about confronting Mike this afternoon," Abby ventured.

"Yeah, I guess that could be it, too. I've been dreading it all week."

"You sure you don't want me to cancel with Birdie? I could call her—"

"And do what? Stick around here all morning hovering over me?" Neal gave a forced smile. "Go on to your brunch, Mom. I'll take some Pepto, get a shower, and be good as new by the time you get back."

"OK. I'll be home by one-thirty. Promise."

The bathroom door closed again. Abby waited until she heard the shower running, then went downstairs and into the kitchen.

Mama was up and dressed, sitting at the kitchen table with a glass of orange juice and the newspaper. She glanced up as Abby entered and smiled. "I'm just looking at the movie listings," she said. "Thought maybe we ought to have a little fun tonight."

Abby sat down at the table. "Are you sure you're strong enough to do something like that? Perhaps we should check with the doctor."

"Never mind the doctor. I feel fine."

"Well, you certainly *seem* fine. You've been making amazing progress with the physical therapy, Mama. And your speech is much clearer."

"Almost feel like my old self again," she said. "Or maybe an *older* version of my old self."

"That's wonderful." Abby patted her hand. "But I think we're going to have to reschedule that movie. Neal Grace is a little under the weather."

A curious look passed over her mother's face. "What do you mean, 'under the weather'?"

"She's got a stomach virus or something. If you ask me, I think she's just nervous about breaking up with this guy she's been dating."

"Mike."

Abby shot her a glance. "You know about him?"

"Neal told me a day or two after I came home from the hospital. Can't say I'm impressed with what I've heard."

"Me either. I offered to cancel my brunch date with Birdie, but she said no. Maybe you could check on her later."

"I will."

"She's really come around, hasn't she, Mama? It's like we've got our old Neal Grace back again."

"Yes. Our old Neal Grace."

Abby thought she saw a shadowed sadness in her mother's expression. But she didn't have time to pursue it at the moment.

⁓

"Just *talk* to him, Abby. I'm sure he didn't mean it the way it sounded."

Abby toyed with her eggs Benedict and thought about Birdie's advice. She had told Birdie about the discussion with Charles the night Mama had been taken to the hospital, and how distressed she was at the idea of putting Mama into a nursing home. Maybe Birdie was right. Maybe he hadn't meant to be so dogmatic about it. At the end of the conversation he had relented, after all, and had not brought up the subject again in any of their conversations in the past couple of weeks.

Of course she *had* been occupied with Mama and Neal Grace lately. She hadn't been alone with Charles since that night in the visitors' lounge. And she couldn't rid her mind of the image of him taking over, being so adamant about decisions "they" needed to make together.

"He thinks you're avoiding him, you know," Birdie confided.

"I'm not avoiding anything. I've been busy."

"Too busy to see your fiancé?" Birdie raised one eyebrow and pointed at Abby's bare left hand. "Or to remember to wear his engagement ring?"

"Too busy to get it sized," Abby corrected archly. "I'll get it done. Soon." She averted her eyes and gazed out the window.

The restaurant—Birdie's choice—was a tiny place on Wall Street, with a bakery in front and a café in back. Next to their table, large windows looked down on a brick plaza sandwiched between the city buildings. Below, in the courtyard, a small crowd had gathered. Abby peered between the leaves of a russet-colored oak tree that stood next to the window. "I wonder what's going on out there?"

"What's going on *in here* is someone trying to avoid my questions," Birdie cracked.

Abby didn't respond. She couldn't speak around the lump in her throat.

She had seen him, just a glimpse. A fiddler, sitting on the stone wall surrounding the massive oak tree. Through the glass she couldn't hear the music, but it filled her mind nevertheless, twining through her consciousness like a familiar, much-loved voice.

Devin Connor.

⌒

Her left side was getting stronger, but the climb up the stairs was still a painful and arduous journey. Edith paused at the landing to catch her breath. *I should have packed a lunch,* she thought wryly.

With some effort she made it to the upstairs hallway and shuffled toward Neal Grace's room. The bedroom door stood ajar, and Edith could see her granddaughter propped up in bed, reading. She pushed it open the rest of the way and knocked on the doorframe. "Care for some company?"

Neal jumped. "Granny Q! What are you doing up here?"

"Coming to visit you, if that's all right."

"You shouldn't be climbing the stairs."

Edith shrugged. "It's therapy. Needed the exercise."

"Well, come on in." Neal got out of bed, dumped an armload of dirty clothes out of a chair onto the floor, and pulled the chair closer. "Sorry the place is such a wreck."

Edith settled herself in the chair while Neal climbed back onto the bed to sit cross-legged with her back up against the headboard.

"Your mother said you weren't feeling well."

"My stomach was upset earlier this morning, but I'm doing better now."

"Throwing up helped, did it?"

Neal shrugged. "Guess I had a bug or something. Mom thinks it's because I'm nervous about breaking up with Mike."

Edith tilted her head. "Does she?"

"That's what she said."

"And what do *you* think?"

Neal averted her eyes and picked at a

loose string on the comforter. "I don't know what you mean."

Edith leaned forward and stilled the girl's fidgeting hands. "Neal Grace, look at me."

Neal raised her head. The expression of misery in her eyes was enough to break any grandmother's heart.

"Tell me more about this young man you've been seeing."

"What about him?" Neal's voice came out as barely a whisper.

"Do you love him?"

"No. I thought I did, I guess. Maybe. I—" She blinked furiously to keep the tears at bay.

"You've had terrible losses and unspeakable pain," Edith finished, working hard to articulate her thoughts. "And in the midst of that pain, you reached out for something. You—"

"I don't want to talk about him," Neal interrupted.

"I know you don't," Edith said gently. "But I expect it's time for such a conversation." She waited for a moment or two, and when Neal didn't respond, she went on. "You've lost a great deal in your brief life, my dear. First your Grandpa Sam, then your father, then me."

"I didn't lose you. You're still here." Neal Grace's voice quivered. "You're not going to die, are you?"

Edith chuckled. "Not today. I hope to be around for quite a few more years. But when I had the stroke, things changed. I changed. The relationship between us changed."

"That was all my fault," Neal muttered. "I should have been able to see that you were still the same person underneath."

"Hindsight's always clearer," Edith said. "I've had the same problem myself recently. Took quite some doing to enable me to see beyond my own clouded vision. But let me finish, if you don't mind."

Neal nodded for her to continue.

"When we see what we love slipping away from us, we tend to grab on to anything that seems to promise a measure of security, of hope."

"Like Mike?"

"Yes, exactly like Mike. Romance, emotional connection—even with the wrong person—can be powerfully seductive. Makes us feel beautiful, desirable, needed. Gives us a sense of belonging when we feel dis—" she paused, concentrating on the word—"dislocated. It can even make us forget the greater wisdom we've accumulated in the course of living."

"What you're saying is that people in love can be stupid."

"Even people not in love. Even people who only *want* to be in love."

Neal shut her eyes and took a deep breath. "Go on."

"And when we get caught up in that sense of belonging," Edith continued, speaking slowly and deliberately, "we can lose sight of who we really are. We can do things we never intended to do."

Neal Grace's eyes snapped open. "Such as?"

Edith gazed into her granddaughter's face. For a brief moment her mind cast back to the child's birth, when she had stood in the hospital room with the squirming, squalling infant in her arms, breathed on her, calmed and comforted her. "Why don't *you* tell *me*?"

All the blood drained from Neal's face, and she froze in place, still as an alabaster statue and almost as white. She swallowed hard, took two or three deep breaths. Then she said, in a voice so small it could have belonged to a child, "I think you already know."

"Maybe," Edith said. "But I believe you need to tell me anyway."

⁓

Never in all her seventeen years had Neal imagined having a conversation like this with her seventy-five-year-old grandmother. She was terrified, mortified. Yet she knew Granny Q was right. She needed to talk about it.

Once she got started, it came fairly easily, despite her apprehensions. Her grandmother sat there, listening compassionately, not interrupting, not challenging her or showing any sign of shock or outrage. Granny Q was pretty cool, she had to admit.

Neal started at the beginning—how claustrophobic she had felt after Daddy's death and Granny Q's stroke. How she had wished for her life to be different, and desperately needed change. How she had known from the beginning that the relationship with Mike was all wrong, but had rationalized until somehow it had begun to seem right. How she had even endured verbal abuse and violent anger because she felt stuck.

Then, suddenly, she realized where this line of thought was taking her. She couldn't go there—not with Granny Q, not with anyone. She stopped talking and sank back against the bedpost.

"Go on," her grandmother said.

Neal shrugged and looked away. "That's about it."

"You sure? Absolutely certain? I got a feeling there's something else. Something you need to say." Her grandmother shook her head. "Confession's only helpful if you tell it all."

"We're Protestants," Neal joked, trying to divert the conversation. "We don't believe in confession."

"We don't go to the church, sit inside a confessional, and speak to a priest through a screen," Granny Q corrected. "Maybe we ought to. Sometimes I think it's easy to confess only to God, who already knows it anyway. Release comes when you don't have to live with keeping secrets from the people you love."

But the people you love can reject you if you've screwed up too much, Neal thought.

As if she had read her granddaughter's mind, Granny Q squared her shoulders and looked intently into Neal's eyes. "There's nothing you could possibly tell me that would make me love you less."

A heavy weight pressed in on her lungs so that Neal could barely breathe. Her hands trembled, and she was afraid she might be sick again. "I'm so ashamed," she whispered.

"Ashamed of having sex with him," Granny Q said. It was not a question.

Neal jerked her head up. "How long have you known?"

"Long enough. I suspect you're also ashamed of getting involved with someone like him in the first place."

"Oh, yeah." Neal bit her lip. "But he didn't force me. And I didn't resist. I didn't enjoy it much, but I didn't say no."

"So what happens now?"

Neal exhaled heavily. "Now I get on with my life and try not to let this experience scar me forever, I guess. This afternoon I'll tell him to get lost, and it'll be over. End of story."

"Is it?"

"Is it what?"

"Is it the end of the story?"

"You bet it is. I don't want to have anything to do with him. Ever again."

She looked up to see Granny Q gazing at her, her expression a mixture of love and pain. "Have you checked the calendar lately?"

Neal did a double take. "What calendar?"

"The calendar that tells you how long it's been since your last cycle."

Her grandmother's face began to swim, as if she were underwater. Neal's mind raced as she counted backward. Six weeks. Maybe seven. The nervous stomach. The queasiness. The nausea.

No, she couldn't possibly be—

But she was. Despite her resistance, at some deep level she knew it was true.

Her voice failed her, and she could barely whisper, "Oh, God, please—no!"

Granny Q hoisted herself up onto the bed, took Neal into her arms, and began to stroke her hair. All the memories from childhood came rushing back, times she had fallen off her bike or cut herself or scraped a tender place on her heart.

She felt herself shrinking, growing younger, becoming a little girl again. A little girl who wanted nothing more than for her grandmother to take the pain away.

"It'll be all right," Granny Q said, her voice quiet and entreating. "We haven't been down this path before, but we'll do it together. You won't be alone."

But Neal knew this wasn't a skinned knee that could be healed with a kiss and a Band-Aid. In a single devastating moment of awareness, she realized a terrible truth.

Her childhood was over . . . forever.

21

More Decisions

By the time her mother's car pulled up in the driveway, Neal had showered and dressed, ridden her bicycle to the drugstore for a home test, and confirmed the fact that she was, indeed, pregnant. Now she sat with her grandmother at the kitchen table and waited as her mother opened the door, saw them and waved, and made her way toward them through the living and dining rooms.

"I'm scared," Neal whispered.

Her grandmother patted her hand. "It'll be all right. I promise."

"Birdie found the greatest new place for brunch," Mom was saying as she approached the kitchen. "We should go sometime. I had eggs Benedict, and Birdie got the pecan waffles. It's down on Wall Street next to—"

She stopped and stared at the two of them. "What's up?"

When neither answered, she put her hands on her hips and grinned. "Come on, out with it. What are you two conspiring about?" She came to the table, leaned over, and felt Neal's forehead with her wrist. "How's that stomach virus, honey? You look better."

"I'm OK," Neal said.

"Did you get something to eat?" She went to the refrigerator and looked inside. "There's leftover chicken. I could make chicken salad sandwiches if anyone's hungry."

"Abby, sit down," Granny Q commanded. "Nobody's hungry, and we need to talk."

Neal took a deep breath and tried to steady herself as her mother returned to the table and sat down.

"It's almost two," her mother said. "Won't Mike be here any minute?"

"Mike's not coming," Neal said. "I called him and postponed. I can't face him right now." *I don't really want to face you, either,* she thought. But she didn't say it.

"I know you've been nervous about

breaking up with him, but putting it off won't make it any easier. Maybe—"

"Mom, please—" Neal interrupted. "Please, just listen."

⌒

Edith sat in silence while Neal Grace began to stumble her way through her confession. She prayed silently that her granddaughter would have the courage to say what had to be said, and that her daughter would have the grace to hear it without condemnation. She had raised Abby to be a loving, empathetic person, but Edith also knew that it was easier to be understanding from a distance, when one's own offspring and future weren't directly involved. This situation was going to demand a great deal of up-close and personal compassion.

"What I'm trying to tell you, Mom," Neal Grace was saying, "is that Mike and I—well, we slept together."

Abby went white. "You slept together," she repeated. "I'm assuming you don't mean taking a nap in the same bed."

"We made love," Neal said. And then, before her mother could respond, she corrected herself. "No. We didn't make love. We had sex."

"Did he force you? You said he had a bad temper—"

Edith opened her mouth to intervene. Of course Abby would be looking for an excuse, some reason she could wrap her mind around. She couldn't imagine that her daughter would ever willingly do something like this.

"It wasn't rape, if that's what you're asking. I agreed to it. It was a stupid thing to do, but I have to take responsibility for my part in it."

"That's very—uh, mature," Abby said, obviously groping for words and trying to keep a lid on her emotions. "But I don't quite understand. I thought we had talked about all this, Neal. About not taking sex lightly, about waiting . . ."

"Yeah," Neal Grace said.

Abby exhaled heavily. "Well, I'm glad you told me. I don't want any secrets between us. And it's clear you regret what you've done. I can only hope you've learned from your mistake, and—"

Edith closed her eyes and shook her head. She supposed it was too much to ask that Abby could completely avoid launching into Mother Mode. "Abby—," she began.

But Abby wasn't listening. "I know you're aware of these things, but I'm going to say them anyway because I'm your mother," she said to Neal Grace. "This could have been much worse, you know. If you'd had unprotected sex, you might have contracted—"

"Abby!" Edith shouted.

Her daughter stopped speaking and turned to look at her as if she'd lost her mind. "What is it, Mother? We're in the middle of a conversation here."

"A conversation has *two* sides." Edith fixed her with a glare. "Let Neal Grace finish."

"I thought she *was* finished. What else is there?" She turned back to her daughter. "Neal?"

Neal Grace was staring down at the table, her fingernail tracing the spot where she had carved her initials when she was ten.

"Neal?" Abby repeated.

Neal looked up. "Mom, we didn't always have protected sex. I'm . . . I'm—"

Abby's gaze flitted from Neal to Edith and back again.

"I'm pregnant."

A silence descended over the kitchen. Edith could hear the faint buzz of the clock on the oven.

"No," Abby breathed.

"Yes."

"You can't be. You're not even eighteen years old."

"I'm old enough to have a baby, Mom."

"How did this happen?"

The tension in the room had been strung as tight as a piano wire. With Abby's question, it snapped, and Edith began to laugh. "How'd it *happen?*" she repeated. "I distinctly recall having an extended conversation with you about the facts of life when you were eleven years old. Do we need a refresher course at this late date?"

Abby was not amused. "I wasn't talking about biology, Mama. As you know perfectly well." She turned back to Neal Grace. "Is it possible you're just late?"

Neal shook her head. "I took a home pregnancy test this morning. It was positive."

"I can't believe it."

"I couldn't believe it, either," Neal muttered. "But it's true."

Abby shut her eyes and pressed a hand to her mouth. "What are you going to do?"

"I believe what your mother is asking," Edith said quietly, "is what are we going to do?"

Abby looked up and gazed into Edith's eyes. "Of course," she agreed. "We're in this together."

"Yes and no," Neal countered. "I mean, I appreciate the support you're trying to give me and all that, but there are some decisions I need to make myself."

Edith gazed at her granddaughter. She seemed braver now, more resolute, as if the very act of telling the truth had roused some inner strength deep in her soul.

"As I see it," Neal went on, "I have four options. First, I could marry Mike. He's already asked me to live with him. He's not real thrilled about the idea of marriage, but with a baby on the way, he might change his mind."

She paused and looked away, then rushed on as if determined to finish before she lost her courage. "Second, I could have an abortion. End of baby. End of problem."

Abby opened her mouth to interrupt. Edith kicked her under the table. She shut her mouth again.

"Third, I could have the baby and give it up for adoption once it's born. And fourth, I could have the baby and keep it."

She stopped speaking, put her head in both hands, and began to massage her temples. Edith watched her granddaughter struggle and felt her own heart breaking. The girl was little more than a child herself. And now, because of one mistake, her whole future had been turned on its axis, her dreams and hopes diverted. College. Dating. Falling in love. Planning a career. Getting married. All the experiences a young woman should be able to enjoy without the pressure and responsibility of caring for a child.

She looked across the table at her daughter. Abby's hopes for Neal Grace's future had gone up in flames, too. She could see it on Abby's face—the loss, the grief, the confusion and agony.

Abby met her gaze, her expression thoroughly miserable, her eyes glazed with unshed tears. She lifted her shoulders in a gesture of helplessness.

Edith laid a hand on her granddaughter's arm. "Are you ready to talk about those options?"

Neal Grace looked up. "I guess so." Her countenance took on a hard, determined expression. "You might as well know right up front that I have no intention of marrying Mike Damatto."

For the first time since the kick under the table, Abby spoke. "Well, that's a relief."

Neal turned to her. "Really? I thought you might try to talk me into getting married— you know, so I'd be respectable, so my baby would have a father and a name."

"Absolutely not," Abby said. "From what you've told me today of that boy, he's a loser and a jerk and a potential wife-beater. No daughter of mine is going to marry someone like that, not as long as I have breath in my lungs to protest." She waved a finger in Neal Grace's face. "And believe me, I am trusting that the genes you've inherited from this family will be very, very dominant."

Neal Grace grinned. "I'll do my best, Mom."

"And since I seem to be on a roll here,"

Abby continued, "let's talk about Option #2."

"Just chill, Mom," Neal Grace said. "I'm not going to have an abortion any more than I'm going to marry Mike."

Abby looked up. "But you said—"

"I said it was an option. A possibility. I have to consider all my alternatives, don't I, even if I reject them?" She ran a hand through her hair. "I . . . I just couldn't do it. On the surface it feels like it might be easier in the long run—one trip to the clinic and bam! Problem solved. I bury the secret, get on with my life, go to college, meet a nice guy. But I don't think I could live with myself if I made that choice."

She looked up into her mother's eyes. "You must be terribly disappointed in me."

Abby sighed. "Honey, I'm disappointed *for* you. For the price you will have to pay."

"So if I don't marry Mike and don't get an abortion, I've got two remaining options," Neal continued. "To keep the baby or give it up for adoption. Either way, it's going to be very difficult—not just for me, but for you and for Granny Q as well."

"And how will you make that decision?" Edith asked.

"I don't know," Neal admitted. "And I may not know for a while." She rubbed a hand over her eyes. "I'm sorry for all of this. I wish I could go back, do things differently, change what's happened."

"No one can change the past," Abby said. "We can only do our best with the present and try to make the future better."

Her daughter's words triggered something in Edith's mind—memories of Grandma Gracie and her own mother, Abigail, of herself as a child, of Sam and little Abby and Gracie's parting words. She saw herself in middle age, holding her fretful infant granddaughter, calming her, easing her into a noisy, frightening new world. And she saw something else, too—a vision of the great-grandchild who was to come, cradled in the same way, loved and protected by her old Great-Granny Q.

She had been left here for a reason. And at this moment, with a clarity that reverberated through her soul, Edith knew what that reason was. She couldn't change the past, but God willing, she might be able to help change the future.

22

Rethinking Everything

Abby got in the car and began to drive—
blindly, aimlessly.

She had to be alone, had to think.

It all seemed like a nightmare—a strange,
bizarre dream. Her daughter, her little girl—
not yet eighteen, still in high school. Unmarried. Pregnant. While they were talking
at the kitchen table, she had managed to
keep her emotions in check. Now everything inside her seemed to be breaking
loose, flying out in all directions, and she
couldn't bring any order to the chaos.

She turned the conversation over in her
mind. Neal Grace had seemed so small, so
terrified and timid when she first began to
talk, but as the truth had come out, she had
seemed to mature right before Abby's eyes.
Somehow, in the midst of a very frightening
and confusing situation, her little girl had

found the strength and courage to think through her options rationally, to begin to make plans.

Thank God, she had rejected the notion of marrying this Mike Damatto character. And she had also rejected the idea of an abortion.

Abby berated herself. Why hadn't she seen what was happening? Skipping school. Dating an older guy. Why had she allowed herself to be so absent from her daughter's life? Why hadn't she picked up on any clues?

Neal Grace had no idea how much commitment was involved in raising a child. She didn't know that a mother never retired, that there was no end to the worry and anxiety and responsibility. And what if she did choose to give the baby up for adoption? Abby couldn't begin to imagine what kind of agonizing pain and long-term guilt her daughter might have to face.

Suddenly Abby realized she was high up on the Parkway. October was in full glory, and the road was clogged with leaf-lookers—cars with out-of-state plates, motorcycles, RVs big as houses. The mountainsides that spread out all around her glowed with red and yellow and orange hues. Sandwiched between an overcrowded minivan and a pickup truck towing a pop-up camper, she glanced at the speedometer and saw that it read twenty-five. Her hands tapped anxiously on the steering wheel. "Enough of this," she muttered to herself. Given the frayed condition of her nerves, she was in no condition to be driving. She'd either end up with an expensive ticket for tailgating or make a spectacular nosedive and crash to her death off one of these precipitous ridges.

She passed through a curved tunnel and, at the next overlook, parked the car and got out. A chilly breeze blew up from the valley, and she shivered. But it wasn't just from the cold. It was, at least in part, from her apprehension at what lay ahead.

Neal Grace had made it clear that she would neither marry Mike nor abort the infant he had fathered. But beyond that, she had made no decisions. How agonizing would it be, Abby wondered, to hold her first grandchild and then abandon it into someone else's arms? And how much more difficult, at her age, to take on even the partial obligation of helping to raise a fatherless infant?

As Abby gazed out over the fall foliage, her eyes unfocused, transforming the mountain scenery into a stunning impressionistic painting. But even as her brain registered the sensory images, her conscious mind was miles away.

She had prayed for change, had wished for a simpler, less burdened life with fewer responsibilities. Briefly she wondered if God, in some kind of cosmic stand-up routine, received her prayers, evaluated them, and answered them with exactly the opposite of what she had asked for.

Or was it a test? A pop quiz to see how much she had learned, how much she could bear?

If it was a test, what in the name of all that was holy was she supposed to learn from it? That prayer was a joke, and that the Almighty couldn't care less about her needs?

That wasn't the attitude toward God that had been drilled into her by Mama and Nana and Great-Grandma Gracie. They had all believed. They had trusted God, had seemed to find meaning in concepts like grace and mercy and faithfulness. They had, from everything Abby had seen, *experienced* the truth they espoused.

Her own approach to faith wasn't that simple. Or perhaps it was *too* simple. Maybe what she called faith was merely wishful thinking—blowing out birthday candles, watching for the first star in the night sky, touching the Wishing Jar for luck.

Abby looked around. The last carload of tourists had pulled out of the parking space, and for the moment she was alone. She went to the edge of the overlook and sat on the low stone wall with her back to the road and her feet in the grass. The breeze had died down, and a warm October sun bathed her face.

"God," she said aloud, her voice tight and hesitant in her own ears, "I don't know how to handle all of this. Mama seems to be doing so well with it, taking it in stride, supporting Neal Grace. I love my daughter and want to do the best for her, but I can't even figure out what the best is. I could use a little help here."

She fell silent. Behind her she could hear the whiz of tires on the Parkway. High in a tree that rose up to her right, a bird was singing. Below, in the valley between two mountain ridges, a hawk coasted on the updraft in a slow, lazy spiral. From somewhere far away, she could just make out the sound of rushing water.

It all reminded her of something she had experienced before. The spectacular long-distance vista. The soothing hush of a creek cascading over rocks. The rustling of small animals amid fallen leaves. Deer grazing beside a pond. An unaccountable sense of peace and well-being.

Devin Connor's place.

~

Neal had a nagging feeling that she ought to give herself more time to think this through, but she couldn't wait. Although she wasn't sure what she was going to do about the baby, she was absolutely certain of one thing: even though she dreaded facing him, she wanted Mike Damatto out of her life. Now. And so, against her grandmother's warnings and T. J.'s resistance, she had decided to go out looking for him.

Telling T. J. about the baby had simply confirmed what Neal had known for a long time. She couldn't ask for a better best friend. Teej had listened without interrupting, refrained from saying "I told you so," and avoided any mention of Neal's neglect of their friendship during the time she had been dating Mike. When Neal had finished, T. J. had shrugged. "OK. Whatever you need, I'm here for you."

What Neal needed at the moment was a ride. T. J. borrowed her mom's car and drove Neal around until they found Mike's Harley parked in front of the Woodside Tavern, a dilapidated bar-and-grill on the west side of town.

"You are *not* going in there alone," T. J. protested when Neal opened the passenger's door.

"I've been here before," Neal said. "It's not as bad as it looks." Despite the fact that her heart was pounding like a jackhammer, she forced a smile. "All right, so it's only a little less disgusting inside. But I need to do this by myself." She held the door open a moment longer. "Wish me luck."

"Are you sure you won't let me go in with you?" T. J. asked. "I don't like the look of this place."

"No, I'll be OK. I don't know how long it will take. I hope it'll be quick, but—"

"Doesn't matter." T. J. put the car in park and shut off the engine. "Just go, OK? I'll be here when you come out."

Neal hesitated. "Lock the doors."

"In a classy neighborhood like this?" T. J. grinned. "Go on. Get this over with, and I'll buy you a burger. Someplace clean."

"You're the best," Neal said.

"I am. And don't you forget it."

Neal shut the car door, squared her shoulders, and clenched her jaw. The thirty-foot walk from the parking lot to the entrance of the bar seemed like thirty miles. Twice she almost lost her nerve and turned back. But at last she pulled the door open and stepped inside.

It took a minute or two for her eyes to adjust to the dim light. Cigarette smoke swirled around her in a gray haze, even though the place was almost empty. A country song was playing on the jukebox—Garth Brooks, Neal thought. *I got friends in low places.* "Yeah, Garth," she muttered under her breath, "me, too."

The bartender recognized her. "You meetin' that man of yours?" he yelled over the music. "He's in the back, playing pool."

Neal nodded and waved and snaked her

way through the maze of tables and chairs into the pool hall. The room was large, with a stained cement floor and three pocket billiard tables in the center. A waist-high bar with stools ran along one wall.

The light was better in here, and she spotted Mike immediately, leaning over the center pool table to attempt a shot into the corner pocket. He made the shot, but scratched, and came up cursing the ball, the table, his opponent, everything in sight. His buddy poked him with a cue stick and pointed in Neal's direction.

Mike turned. "Well, hey baby," he slurred in a breathy voice, a bad imitation of Elvis. He had been drinking. Neal had anticipated that but hadn't expected him to be this far gone at four in the afternoon.

She motioned him over. "I need to talk to you. Someplace private."

"Oh yeah," he said, turning up a half-smile in her direction. He looked over his shoulder toward his friend. "Take a hike, Pete," he said. "My woman wants *privacy.*"

Pete threw down the pool cue and stalked into the bar, muttering about getting back the money he had lost to Mike.

"Sore loser," Mike said when he was gone. "Can't shoot pool worth—"

"Mike," Neal interrupted. "I need your attention."

"Sure, I'll give you attention." He began backing her into a corner. "All the attention you want." He started touching her, running his hands over her body, grabbing at her. "Knew you'd come back," he mumbled. "Knew you couldn't stay away."

She tried to make him listen, but he kept talking over her. "I'll give you what you want, babe. Just me and you."

"No, Mike," she said, pushing him away. "There is no me and you. It's over."

"Over?" he eased off a little, looking dazed. "What do you mean, over?"

"I can't see you again. We're finished."

"You don't know what you're saying." He turned aside and picked up a glass of beer from the bar, then retrieved the cue stick and waved it. "Come on, have a drink. Let's play some pool."

"I don't want a drink."

"Sure you do." He leaned close and pressed the rim of the glass to her lips. "Drink up. Let's have a little fun, babe."

"Stop it!" Neal jerked away. The glass

slipped out of his hand and smashed to splinters across the concrete floor.

"See what you done?" he yelled. "You made me spill a perfectly good beer! Why, I ought to—"

"You ought to listen for once, Mike," she said evenly. "I have to tell you something. It's important."

He glared at her. "What's so important that it's worth losing my beer?"

Neal shut her eyes. "Mike, I'm pregnant."

There was a long silence. When Neal looked up again, he was staring at her with his mouth hanging open. "You're kidding."

"No. And since you're the only person I've ever been with—"

His face contorted into a mask of rage. Those sleepy eyes, which Neal had once thought so smoldering and sexy, took on a dark and ominous expression. A muscle in his jaw twitched. He took a step forward, forcing her back against the bar, and when he spoke again, his voice was tight and menacing. "You conniving little b—"

"Mike, wait," she interrupted. "You don't understand. I'm not asking for anything from you. I just thought you ought to know, that's all."

He didn't hear her. "I shoulda known when you said you wanted to get married that you'd pull something like this!" he yelled. "Had it all planned, didn't you? Get pregnant and trap me into—"

"I'm not trapping you into *anything!*" Neal shouted back, raising her voice to be heard over his tirade.

The skin under his stubble of beard went pale, then flushed red. He lifted the pool cue and slammed it down on the bar. "You'll pay for this, you scheming little tramp. Nobody takes advantage of Mike Damatto. *Nobody!*"

She felt the wood of the bar pressing into the small of her back. He swung the cue before she could duck and caught her on the left side of the head. She saw flashing lights, and the room began to sway. He hit her again, a glancing blow just as she fell.

Dazed, Neal pulled her knees up to her chest to ward off the kicks he was aiming at her midsection. She could hear scuffling, could see shadowy images of feet and legs.

"Mike, cut it out! Let her go!"

The bartender's shout sliced through the confusion, the voice of an avenging angel come to save. Someone pulled her attacker away—his friend Pete, she thought. When she dared to look up, Mike was caught, struggling to free himself. The bartender, who was burly enough to have doubled as a bouncer, had Mike's arms pinned behind him. "Call the police," he said to Pete. "Tell them to send an ambulance, too."

Neal got slowly to her feet. Her forehead was bleeding, but she didn't think the gash was deep. "Forget it," she said. "I'm all right."

"Yeah, but you want to press charges against this jerk, don't you?"

Neal shook her head. "Not this time."

The bartender wrenched Mike's arms until he cried out in pain. "You lucked out, Damatto. Don't ever lemme see you in here again. You got it?" He twisted harder.

"Yeah, yeah," Mike snarled.

"Good. Now get outta here before I call the cops and sign a complaint myself." He shoved Mike toward the exit. Pete followed him, casting an apologetic glance in Neal's direction.

When they were gone, the bartender led Neal out of the poolroom and settled her gently at a table near the door. "Are you all right, Miss?"

Neal managed a faint smile, calmed by his polite formality. "Yes, I think so."

"Let me get you a drink, or something to eat. We got great sandwiches. On the house."

"Just a Coke, please."

The bartender left and returned a few minutes later with the Coke, a clean bar towel, and a glass of ice. As Neal sipped her drink, he applied ice to the wound and cleaned the blood from her face.

Neal looked at him. "What's your name?"

"Angelo," the man replied.

"Angelo," Neal mused. "Figures."

He blushed and ducked his head. "I ain't no angel, Miss, if that's what you're thinking. You can ask my mama if you don't believe me."

"You were for me." Neal took a deep breath. "Thanks for helping, Angelo. You may have saved my life."

"Don't have no respect for any man hits a woman," he said gruffly. "If ya don't mind me asking, what's—"

"What's a nice girl like me doing in a place like this?" Neal chuckled.

"Well, yeah, that too. But I was gonna ask, what's a girl like you doing with a butthead like Damatto."

Neal shook her head. "Temporary insanity." She finished her Coke and fished in her purse. "Sure I can't pay you?"

"Naw, forget it," he said. "How you gonna get home?"

"I got a friend waiting for me."

At the thought of T. J. outside in the parking lot, Neal cringed. If Teej ever had the inclination to say *I told you so,* this was her big chance.

~

Abby pulled up in front of Devin Connor's cabin and got out of the car. The afternoon was beginning to fade, and long shadows stretched across the pond and into the woods behind the cabin.

She had taken no more than two steps toward the door, and was just rethinking the wisdom of coming here, when Devin's golden retriever barreled out of the woods barking. He came to her immediately, poking his nose into her hand and sidling up to her to be petted.

"Hello, Mozart." She knelt down to greet him, stroking his silky ears.

"With Mo around, I don't need a doorbell, do I?"

Abby raised her head. Devin Connor stood to one side of the path, backlit by a slant of sunlight, and her heart did a little flip. She struggled awkwardly to her feet.

"Come in," he offered. "I'll make us some coffee."

"No, I—" She groped for an explanation. "I was just driving by, and—"

Devin came closer. "Nobody just *happens* to drive by here," he said with a faint smile. "Come inside and sit, and you can tell me what's on your mind."

Twenty minutes later, Abby was sipping at her second cup of coffee and toying with a third cookie. She had told him about her engagement to Charles, about Neal Grace's pregnancy, about her own confusion and mixed emotions—everything.

He had made it easy. He never once expressed shock, hadn't asked why she was coming to him after such a long stretch of silence between them—and about something so personal. Nor had he given so much as a hint of disapproval about anything she said. He had simply listened, nodding, holding eye contact, touching her arm once or twice.

"Mama's handling this much better than I am," Abby confessed. "She's so—*strong.*"

"And you think you're not?"

"I feel completely overwhelmed, Devin. If Neal Grace does decide to keep the baby, I'll support her, of course, but it's so much *responsibility.* I thought . . . I thought my life was about to become simpler, less complicated."

He gazed into her eyes. "And that's why you agreed to marry Charles—to uncomplicate your life."

Abby nodded. "Partly, I guess. I thought if I had someone to share the burden with, it wouldn't seem so . . . so—"

"Burdensome?" He smiled.

"Yes. Charles is a good man. He's stable and secure. It makes sense for me to marry him. He would take on a lot of the responsibility I've been shouldering for so long, and—"

"Abby?"

She stopped fidgeting with her napkin and looked up. "What?"

"Have you told Charles about Neal Grace's baby?"

"Not yet. I . . . I'm a little apprehensive about telling him, I'll admit. He has very definite opinions about what kinds of decisions we should make for the future. And I'm afraid—" She stopped, unable or unwilling to articulate what she was feeling.

"Afraid of what his reaction might be?" Devin said softly.

"Yes. He already wants to put Mama into a nursing home. She can get better care there, he says. He has this ideal image, I think, of what our life together should be like. Just the two of us alone, with Neal Grace off at college and Mama being cared for elsewhere. I can't imagine how he would respond to the idea of a single mother and a new baby in the house."

Abby fell silent, and for a minute or two neither of them spoke. After a moment Devin reached out and took her hand. The contact sent a thrill through her, fire and ice running across her nerves and into her veins. She kept very still, concentrating on maintaining her composure.

"I only have one thing to ask, Abby," he

whispered. "Why are you here telling me instead of there telling him?"

And Abby didn't have the faintest idea how to answer him.

23

Abby's Dilemma

Quinn House
October 31

In a gust of wind October was departing, swirling away in its multicolored cape without a backward glance. Leaves that had so brilliantly clothed the mountainsides only a few weeks ago now lay in soggy brown heaps, and bare tree limbs shivered in the cool late-autumn wind.

Abby sat on the front porch swing, wrapped in a shawl, watching the rain dripping off the eaves. On either side of the top step, two carved pumpkins glowed orange in the gathering dusk.

A buffet was already spread on the kitchen counter—roast beef and carved turkey and crusty French loaves, spinach dip, a pumpkin Bundt cake with orange drizzle frosting, and the iced cutout cookies Neal Grace, T. J., and Mama had spent all afternoon baking and decorating. The table was set with pumpkin-shaped plates and jet-black candles, and the chandelier swathed with fake spider webs. A big plastic jack-o'-lantern full of miniature candy bars sat on the table in the front hallway, ready for trick-or-treaters. Birdie and Taylor would be arriving any minute.

And Charles.

Abby shivered with apprehension. She still hadn't told Charles about Neal Grace's pregnancy, and she couldn't put it off any longer. She had to tell him tonight, no matter what his response might be. Sometime during the evening, she'd get him alone and break the news to him.

The party had been Neal's idea. She had become quite the little homebody, spending much of her after-school time in the kitchen with T. J. and her grandmother. Mama was teaching the girls how to cook. Neal actually made her bed most days, and a week or so ago Abby arrived home from work to find her doing laundry.

Maybe it was hormones. Maybe aliens had abducted her real daughter and left this new Neal Grace in her place. Whatever the case, Abby had decided just to accept things as they were and be grateful.

Lights from a car swung into the driveway, and Abby recognized Birdie's SUV. She got to her feet, her stomach churning, and watched as Birdie and Taylor got out of the front seat. A moment later Charles drove up and emerged from his car.

The three of them dashed through the rain and ran up the stairs to the porch. Charles leaned down to kiss her. Abby turned aside, and his lips grazed her cheek.

"I brought a potato salad," Birdie explained as she handed over a large plastic container. "Hope that's OK." She shook the water off her umbrella and set it in the corner.

"Perfect." Abby hugged her and greeted Taylor. "We're having build-your-own subs with roast beef and turkey."

She ushered them inside. "Neal! Mama! Our guests are here!"

Neal and T. J. came barreling down the stairs from the second floor, and Mama appeared in the kitchen doorway. While Birdie and Taylor were being introduced to T. J.,

Charles grabbed Abby's elbow and steered her back out onto the porch.

"I want to know what's going on," he demanded.

"What do you mean?" Abby attempted an innocent tone but couldn't meet Charles's gaze.

"I mean," he said in a low, deliberate voice, "you've been avoiding talking to me. I know you're hiding something, Abby."

"This is not the time to talk, Charles." Abby edged away from him.

"We haven't been alone together in weeks," he said. "And even when we're together, you're not really *there*. You always seem to be someplace else. If you're having second thoughts about marrying me, I think I should know it."

A tiny, unexpected ray of hope flared to life inside her. "Are *you* having second thoughts?"

"Of course not. But there shouldn't be secrets between us. Something's bothering you, and I think I deserve to know what it is."

Devin Connor's question surfaced in Abby's mind: *Why are you here telling me instead of there telling him?* For the first time since that conversation, Abby had an answer. *Because you feel safe and he doesn't.*

It was an unwelcome revelation—and an unfair assessment, since she hadn't really given Charles a chance. Abby looked up at him. "You're absolutely right," she said. "Later tonight we'll get some time alone and I'll tell you everything."

        ~

Halfway through dinner, the doorbell rang. Abby pushed her chair back from the table. "Trick-or-treaters, probably. I'll get it." She went into the hall, grabbed the bucket of candy, and opened the front door.

It was Devin Connor.

"Hope I'm not interrupting anything." He held out a leather case. "I believe these sunglasses are yours. You left them at the cabin."

Abby stared at him. "You . . . you could have called."

"Yes, I could have. I probably should have, now that I think about it. But I wanted to—" He stopped abruptly, peering past her shoulder into the dining room. "You have

company. I'm sorry to interrupt. I'll be going."

Just then a pod of tiny Power Rangers
swarmed onto the porch, followed by
Winnie the Pooh, Tigger, and Cinderella.
Abby found herself diverted by the task of
handing out candy and complimenting the
children's costumes, and by the time she
waved good-bye to them, Devin had disappeared.

She turned to go back into the house and
felt her knees give way.

He was in the dining room, being ushered
to a chair by Mama, shaking hands with
Taylor and Birdie and . . . and Charles. Neal
Grace was setting a place for him.

All the air rushed out of Abby's lungs. Her
two worlds had just collided.

~

Neal had recognized Devin Connor the moment she spotted him standing at the front
door. Mom had let her read a final draft of
the article about the man who played his
fiddle on the streets of Asheville, and had
shown Neal the photographs she had
taken. Mom had obviously been proud of
that article. But Neal had also seen a

change come over her mother's face whenever she talked about this man. An aliveness, an expression of enthusiasm that went beyond journalistic interest. There was something about him—something Mom wasn't telling.

Now Neal knew what it was. The man wasn't exactly gorgeous, not like Brad Pitt or anything, but he was good-looking, for an older guy. Great smile. Fabulous blue eyes that lit up when he talked. She felt an immediate connection with him. When she drew him into the house, he took her hand, leaned over, and whispered, "Your mom told me about your little miracle. Congratulations." She could have kissed him.

Little miracle. Had anyone else even *thought* about interpreting this pregnancy as something to celebrate? Not a chance. Her condition had been described as a mistake, an "unwanted pregnancy," something to be endured. But Devin Connor, a man she had never met until this moment, intuitively understood what Neal herself had begun to recognize. The mystery of life, growing inside her. Her child. Her baby. No matter what its origins, it was, indeed, a miracle. And at last someone else had affirmed the wonder.

She set a place for him at one end of the table and watched as he created a sandwich of roast turkey, spinach dip, and Swiss cheese. Granny Q was already engaging him in conversation when Mom shut the porch door and came back into the dining room.

Devin looked up. "Your daughter invited me to stay a while," he said. "I hope you don't mind."

Neal watched her mother closely. Her face reddened a bit, but she somehow managed to find her manners. "Of course not," she said, sounding a little shaky. She sank into her seat and began shooting daggers at Neal—the look of silent reprimand only a mother could give.

Neal frowned. What was the big deal about inviting an unexpected guest to join them? There was plenty of food.

She glanced down the table and saw Charles glaring at Mom. So that was it. The man looked positively livid. *He's jealous,* Neal thought.

She turned and smiled brightly at the fiddler. "So, Mr. Connor," she said, "Mom tells us you're quite a good musician. I loved the article about you, by the way."

"Call me Devin," he said. "I haven't seen the article yet, but I'm sure your mother made me seem much wiser and more interesting than I actually am."

"Don't suppose fiddling on the streets is a very lucrative occupation," Charles growled from the other end of the table.

Devin seemed totally oblivious to the attack. "I don't make much money at it, if that's what you're asking," he replied mildly. "But it gives me the opportunity to do what I love."

He turned back toward Neal. "How are you getting along?" he asked. "If my calculations are correct, you'll be graduating before the baby arrives, won't you?"

An icy silence settled over the room. Neal looked at her mother's face, which had gone ashen, and at Charles's, which was beginning to turn red. "Yes," she whispered.

Devin's face broke into that dazzling smile, and he patted her hand. "Isn't it wonderful?" He directed this comment to Charles, who by now had gone from red to purple. "A new baby coming into the world is always a cause for rejoicing, and—"

"Devin—" Neal's mother interrupted in a choked voice. But she didn't have a chance to finish her sentence.

"Abby," Charles demanded, pushing back his chair and standing up. "I'd like to speak to you privately, if you don't mind."

⁓

"A *baby?*" he yelled as Abby followed him into the back hallway that led to her mother's bedroom. "She's going to have a baby?"

"Please, Charles, keep your voice down," Abby pleaded.

"And just when did you intend to fill me in on this insignificant bit of news? Before the kid started school? Or maybe you were planning to wait till he went to college?"

"Charles, I intended to tell you, honestly I did, but—"

"But what? Did you think it would just go away?"

"Of course not. Charles, be reasonable. Try to see it my way. I've been dealing with so much lately, and—"

"And you didn't think it was appropriate to tell your *fiancé* that your daughter got knocked up by some—"

"Stop it!" Abby shouted back. "I won't have you talking about Neal Grace like that."

"Like what?" he whirled around to face her. "Like she's a tramp? And where, may I ask, did she learn such behavior? By watching you with that . . . that fiddler?"

His accusation was like a slap in the face. Abby reeled from the verbal blow. "Devin Connor has nothing to do with this. Nothing! He has never even been in this house until tonight."

"Ah, but you've been in *his* house, haven't you? Long enough to leave your sunglasses there so he'd have to bring them back to you. And I'll bet it wasn't the first time you'd been there, either, was it? *Was it?*"

"No," Abby said in a whisper. "I was there more than once, taking photographs, doing the interview for the magazine—"

"And I'm sure that was *all* you were doing," he challenged, his voice laced with sarcasm.

"Yes. That was all I was doing." It was the truth. There was nothing in Abby's relationship with Devin that she should feel guilty for. Nothing except . . . except . . .

Except her feelings.

As she stood there, watching Charles, listening to him rage out of control, Abby suddenly understood why she had felt safe with Devin and not with her own fiancé. There was a gentleness about Devin, an inner groundedness that enabled him to accept others where they were, as they were. She knew instinctively that no matter what she told him, he would be able to handle it with grace and without condemnation.

"Devin is not the point here," she said at last. "He's a friend, that's all. The point is, I should have told you about Neal Grace's pregnancy."

Charles exhaled a long breath and bit his lower lip. "I accept your apology," he said. "Yes, you should have told me. I have the right, I believe, to be kept in the loop as to what goes on in this family." He leaned against the wall. "Now we just have to figure out what to do about it. Who's the father?"

Abby sank into the chair that sat outside Mama's bedroom door. "The father is out of the picture."

"Well, we're going to get him back in the picture," Charles said firmly. "He's going to marry her, no two ways about it."

"*She's* not going to marry *him,*" Abby countered. "Neal Grace has been perfectly clear about that. And even if she wanted to marry him, I'd be standing in the church door with a baseball bat to make sure it didn't happen. He's an abusive jerk, and he'd make her life miserable."

"All right, then," he conceded. "How far along is she?"

"A few weeks. What difference does that make?"

"Early abortions are much safer than late-term ones."

Abby shook her head. "She's not going to have an abortion, either."

"And who came to this conclusion?"

"Neal did. She might consider giving the baby up for adoption, but although she hasn't said so yet, I think she may be leaning toward keeping the child."

He pushed off the wall and paced down the hall and back. "Abby, listen to me. Do you really think a seventeen-year-old girl is capable of making her own decisions on an issue like this? Doesn't she realize that a baby will ruin her life? Not to mention all *our* plans."

"Our plans?" Abby repeated.

"Yes, our plans. If we're going to be married, Abby, I have a right to some say in this. She doesn't want to marry this guy who knock—who got her pregnant. OK, I can live with that. I can even live with her not getting an abortion, although I still think that's the obvious choice. But if she's determined to have this baby, she *will* give it up for adoption. I'm not going to live the rest of my life as a surrogate father to a kid who isn't even mine. You understand?"

"Yes," Abby said quietly. "I understand."

She understood, all right.

"Good," he went on. "Then we're agreed. Neal Grace will graduate in the spring, have the baby, give it up for adoption, and go on to college as planned in the fall. I've made all the arrangements for your mother, too, and—"

Abby held up a hand. "My mother? What about my mother?"

"I've found just the place for her. Not too far from here, out near Black Mountain. She'll have her own room with a private bath, and you can visit her whenever—"

"Charles," Abby interrupted. "My mother is not going to a nursing home, and my daughter is not going to be forced to give up her baby."

His face went blank. "What are you talking about? I've already told you I won't live in this house with your unmarried daughter and her illegitimate child."

"Yes, you have, Charles. You've made your position very clear."

"Then what—?"

"Then until you can at least pretend to try to see my side of things, this conversation is over." She turned on her heel and walked down the hallway toward the dining room.

He caught up with her at the doorway, grabbed her arm, and wrenched her around to face him. "What do you think you're doing? I thought we understood each other."

"We understand each other perfectly." Abby narrowed her eyes at him. "You want a simple, uncomplicated life, with me all to yourself. You've laid down your self-centered ultimatums and expected me to fall in line. You want me to choose between my family and you. Fine. I'll choose. But don't expect me to choose you."

"Abby, you don't know what you're saying."

"I know exactly what I'm saying."

"We need to talk about this—calmly and rationally, like adults."

It took all of Abby's self-control not to blow him out of the water right then and there. Instead, she inhaled deeply and said, "Perhaps we do. But I'm obviously not able to relate *calmly* and *rationally* at the moment."

She pulled away from him and walked to the dining room doorway. Everyone was sitting rigidly around the table as if they'd been turned to stone. Clearly, they had all overheard the argument in the back hallway.

"Charles has to leave now," Abby said. "If you'll all excuse me, I'll see him to the door."

Aware of all eyes on her back, Abby ushered Charles to the porch without another word and watched until the taillights of his sedan disappeared into the night.

Exhaustion, mingled with immense relief, flooded through her. She shut the front door and leaned against it for a moment, eyes closed, trying to summon the strength to return to the party.

Behind her she heard a confusing clamor of sounds: the scraping of chairs against the hardwood floor, rustling, murmuring.

Then a roar of affirmation. Clapping, cheering, hoots, and whistles.

She opened her eyes and saw that her mother, Neal, T. J., Devin—even Taylor and Birdie—were all on their feet, applauding her.

Neal Grace left the table and came into the front hall, sweeping her into a crushing embrace. And amid the racket, she heard her daughter's whisper in her ear:

"Way to go, Mom."

24

Walking through the Fire

For a long time that night, Abby lay awake, her mind turning over the events of the evening. When the mantel clock downstairs chimed one, she was thinking about Charles Bingham. He wasn't a bad guy, really. With some effort, she might be able to make him see that family was more important than the simple, uncomplicated life he had envisioned. Maybe she should give him another chance.

Or maybe you just think he's your only chance, her mind argued.

Much as she resisted admitting it, there was some truth to that. A fifty-plus widow with an ailing mother and a pregnant teenage daughter didn't have the best of opportunities to find a compatible soul mate. And spending the next thirty years alone certainly wasn't a pleasant prospect.

But did she really want to compromise everything she held dear just for the sake of having someone—anyone—in her life? *You don't have to settle for just anyone,* her mind argued.

An image of Devin Connor hovered behind her closed eyelids. Smiling at her, playing that haunting, unforgettable music on his fiddle.

No. Devin was just a friend. A good friend, she was coming to believe, but no more. So what if a mere glimpse of him made her heart pound? So what if his very presence brought a sense of peace and well-being to her soul? Those were *her* feelings. He had given no indication of reciprocating them. He had simply been . . . kind.

The clock struck two. Abby thrashed around in the bed, unable to get comfortable. She held very still, trying not to think. At last her eyes grew heavy, and her limbs began to relax.

Then, just as she felt herself melting away into sleep, she heard a rustling whisper: *Believe. Hope. Risk.*

Her eyes snapped open. Had she really heard the words? Or was her mind playing tricks on her in that space between waking and sleeping? Believe. Hope. Risk. What on earth did *that* mean?

She turned over and pulled the covers higher. Her mind drifted again, and from somewhere far away she heard a fiddle playing a mournful, familiar tune.

~

The dream was an odd collage of images from her recent waking hours. Charles pleading with her to return to him. Devin's music in the background. An infant crying in another room. A leering jack-o'-lantern face, its features illuminated by a wavering yellow light. Neal Grace shouting, "I told you, Mike, it's over. I'm not getting rid of this baby, and I'm not hooking back up with you."

Abby stirred and turned over. The last part seemed to be reality intruding itself into her dream. She heard the front door slam, then footsteps coming up the stairs.

"Neal?" she called softly.

A shadowy figure appeared in the doorway of the bedroom. "Didn't mean to wake you, Mom. Sorry."

"What time is it?"

"Nearly four."

"What's going on?"

"Mike showed up. Wants me back—but without the baby."

"What did you tell him?"

"I told him to get lost, what else? He seems to think that if I had an abortion, I'd come running back to him and everything would be cool." She sagged against the doorpost. "Of course, he's lost far too many brain cells to be rational."

Abby raised up on one elbow. "Are you all right?"

"Yeah, I'm fine. Go back to sleep."

Neal padded down the hall in her sock feet, and Abby barely heard the bedroom door close before she was drifting again.

The bizarre dream images returned—this time with Charles's face morphing into a jack-o'-lantern that kept growing larger and larger, the flame inside the head rising higher and brighter. She could smell the distinctive scent of charred pumpkin as the candle flame singed the top of the jack-o'-lantern. The baby's crying increased in volume, rising to the level of a scream, a banshee's wail . . .

The bed was shaking.

"Mom!" a voice yelled in her ear. "Mom, wake up!" Someone grabbed her shoulders and shook her, hard.

Abby jerked upright in bed. "What?"

"Come on, Mom—we've got to get out!"

She was fully awake now—she was sure of it. Neal Grace was in her face, shouting. The baby kept on crying, screaming. She could still smell the smoky scent of the candle in the pumpkin—

No. It wasn't a baby, wasn't a candle. It was—

The smoke alarm.

Fire. Real fire.

She gasped and took in a lungful of smoke. In the darkness she could make out a creeping haze overhead, moving downward.

"Get your grandmother!" she cried, lunging out of bed and grabbing her robe off the chair. "Get outside—now!"

Neal Grace bolted for the stairs, and Abby followed close on her heels. When she turned on the downstairs lights, she could see that Mama was already out of bed, holding her hands over her ears and wandering around in the living room, looking dazed and confused. Smoke poured from the direction of the kitchen.

"Granny Q!" Neal yelled as she hit the bottom landing. "Let's go!"

Neal reached Mama first, stationing herself on the old woman's left side and hustling her toward the front door. They made it to the porch just as the kitchen ceiling caved in. Abby, right behind them, turned to look.

It was a horrifying sight—fire raining down from above, licking up from below. And she, like Lot's wife, frozen in place as she witnessed the destruction. She grasped blindly for support, found the key rack on the wall next to the door, held on for dear life.

"Mom, come on!" A hand snaked out and grabbed her, hauling her out onto the porch and into the yard.

Abby looked up. In the second-story windows, she could see flames leaping and dancing. Above the house, in the cold, bright night, a million icy stars speckled the frozen sky. Golden sparks rose up into the blackness to join with the silver ones high overhead.

She looked down at the frosty grass.

Neal Grace had no shoes, and the heavy white sweat socks she wore had wicked up moisture until they were drenched. Abby felt a shiver run through her. She clutched her robe more closely about her and discovered that she held something cold and sharp in her hand.

Her car keys.

Neal saw them and grabbed them from her. "In the car," she commanded, herding Abby and her grandmother toward the driveway. She got in the driver's seat, backed the car a safe distance from the house, and left it idling, the heater running full blast.

Dazed, Abby watched as yellow flames licked out the windows and danced against the red brick of the exterior walls—an eerie performance, as if the house itself were alive. Alive like the phoenix, consumed in its own nest, determined to go down singing . . .

It might have only been a few minutes, sitting in the car, staring through the windshield as both past and present went up in flames, but it seemed like forever. At last the wail of sirens and the blaze of emergency lights cut through the night. Neal Grace got out of the driver's seat and went to assure the EMTs that everyone was all right and no one was in the house.

Despite the firefighter's efforts, the flames burned on, kindled by the dry wood that made up the internal framework of the old structure. Dawn finally broke, revealing little remaining of Quinn House except the stout brick walls, one charred section of the front porch, and a soggy mess of smoking rubble. What hadn't been burned had been flooded.

Abby took in the sight of her ruined ancestral home, and the only question that came to her mind was the unanswerable *Why?* From the backseat of the car, she heard her mother murmuring something else, words she remembered only vaguely from years gone by: "When you pass through the water, I will be with you . . . When you walk through the fire, you shall not be burned."

25

One Last Wish

By eight o'clock in the morning, neighbors had gathered, bringing blankets and quilts, lawn chairs, thermos jugs of coffee, and boxes of donuts. One thoughtful woman even came up with a pair of tennis shoes for Neal Grace.

Abby would not—could not—leave the scene of the destruction. She sat in a folding chair on the sidewalk in front of the house, staring at the ruin, her mind refusing to believe what her eyes could see.

"I . . . I can't think," she said, turning to Neal Grace. "I have no idea what to do now."

"You're in shock, Mom," Neal said. "We'll wait here until the firemen are sure everything's out. Then we'll go rent a hotel room, call the insurance company, get some rest."

"Where's Mama?"

"She's lying down at Mrs. Thornton's next door. She's fine—just a little tired."

Abby shook her head. "I can't imagine what she's feeling right now. She's lived in this house her entire life."

"So have you, Mom," Neal reminded her gently. "It's a horrible loss—for all of us. But the house can be rebuilt. At least we're all alive."

Abby gazed at her daughter in wonder. She seemed so mature, so composed, becoming the comforter in this moment of crisis. It offered Abby a fleeting glimpse of the kind of parent Neal Grace would be, and in that instant Abby devoutly hoped Neal would decide to keep her baby.

Neal turned and looked over her shoulder. "Birdie's here," she said. "And it looks like Charles is driving up right behind her."

Abby bit her lip. "I spent a good part of last night wondering if I should give Charles another chance," she admitted. "Maybe I was too hard on him." Her eyes wandered back to the gutted house. "Maybe we need him right now."

Neal put a hand on her mother's shoulder. "That's your decision, Mom," she said. "Just remember that need isn't a very good foundation for a relationship. I learned that the hard way." She patted her belly and grinned wryly. "I'd better give you some space to talk to him. If you want me, I'll be at the Thorntons', checking on Granny Q."

Birdie jumped out of her SUV, lifted Abby bodily from the lawn chair, and enveloped her in an enormous hug. "I am so, so sorry," she said, her voice choked with tears. "I came as soon as I heard."

Abby leaned back and looked at her. "How *did* you hear?"

"Neal called from the neighbors' house. She said she thought you'd want me to come."

"Of course." Abby bit her lip to keep back the tears. "It's so awful!"

"But everybody's OK, right?" Birdie looked around. "Your mother?"

"She's fine. Resting next door." Abby forced a smile. "In case you hadn't noticed, Neal Grace has taken charge."

"I did notice. She's a great kid." Birdie sat down in one of the chairs and motioned Abby to take a seat. "Listen, I've talked to Taylor. You're welcome to stay with us while—" she motioned toward the burned-out house—"while repairs are being made."

"That's very generous," Abby said, "but you don't have room. I'm guessing the rebuilding will take months. We'll get one of those long-term hotel suites, probably. The insurance will pay for it."

"You sure?"

"Yes, I'm—"

A voice behind her interrupted. "I have a better idea."

Abby turned to see Charles standing in the street a few feet beyond the sidewalk. He was dressed in a white shirt, tie, and wool sport coat—obviously on his way to teach his morning classes.

Birdie stood up. "Three's a crowd," she whispered, giving Abby a kiss on the cheek. "I've got to go, anyway. Come for dinner tonight, all three of you. We'll make plans then."

Charles waited until Birdie drove away, then folded himself into the chair next to Abby.

"I'm sorry about what happened last night," he said, staring at the ground and twisting his fingers together.

"The fire, you mean?"

"No. I mean, yes, I am sorry about the fire. But I was referring to our—" he paused and groped for words—"our misunderstanding."

Abby watched him and waited for him to continue. He was apologizing. And he did seem genuinely sorry. Maybe he was now prepared to be a part of her life as it was, not as he wanted it to be.

"I spent a long time last night thinking about . . . about us," he said. "I do want to marry you. To take care of you."

Something in his tone annoyed Abby, but she couldn't pinpoint the precise source of the irritation.

"Then, this morning, when Birdie called and told me about the fire, I saw everything in a different perspective. It was like a sign."

"A sign?" Abby parroted.

"Yes. Don't you see? You've been burdened far too long. With this house. With caring for your mother. And now Neal Grace's baby."

"Those are not burdens, Charles."

"Of course they are. You told me so yourself. How you wished for a simpler, less complicated life. And now, because of the fire, your wishes can come true."

Abby started to speak, but he held up a hand. "Let me finish, please. Surely after this tragedy you can see the wisdom of finding a safer place for your mother, somewhere she can be looked after. With the insurance money, we could build a house of our own, just right for the two of us. Given the circumstances, I'm sure Neal could stay with her friend T. J. until graduation. We could get married right away, Abby. We can live in my apartment for the time being. Until we get our house built."

Abby stared at him, rendered completely speechless by this twisted interpretation of her life and desires. He saw her as weak and needy, wanting him to take charge, to care for her. And to be honest, Abby had to admit that for a time that was *exactly* what she thought she wanted.

Perhaps she had been unfair to Charles. Perhaps, subconsciously, she had even used him. But how could he fail to understand what she had told him last night? How could he imagine that at such a vulnerable time in her life she would merely hand over the reins to him and let him control the course of her future?

Devin Connor would never do such a

thing. Devin would understand how she felt, and he would help her find her own answers, and support her—and Mama and Neal Grace—in what *they* decided was their best course of action. Devin would—

A bittersweet longing welled up within her as the truth insisted its way into her consciousness. For weeks her rational mind had resisted the idea. Devin was an artist, a philosopher, an unrealistic idealist with no material assets. He scraped together a meager living playing his music on the streets and serving as a caretaker for someone else's property. He had nothing to call his own.

Nothing except character. Faithfulness. Love. Passion for life. A soul at peace. All the things that really counted.

Her mind wrapped around the astonishing awareness: *she was in love with him.*

The moment Abby's consciousness gave way to the admission, an extraordinary transformation began to take hold of her. She sensed it, welling up inside of her—a warmth spreading through her body, an energy, a surge of strength and courage, as if someone had injected adrenaline directly into a vein. She had no idea if Devin could ever feel about her the way she felt about him. But none of that mattered. What did matter was that she felt nothing for Charles Bingham. And whether or not Devin ever loved her in return, she had no intention of marrying a man she did not love in exchange for the security of a less complicated life.

Charles lifted his head and smiled at her, and she could see in his eyes that he didn't have a clue about who she was or what she wanted. "Admit it, Abby. It's a perfect solution."

She gritted her teeth. *Count to ten,* she warned herself silently. *Keep your temper.*

She got as far as eight before the pressure cooker blew.

"You just don't get it, do you?" she said in a low, controlled voice. "You honestly think that all you have to do is snap your fingers, present your well-devised plan, and I'll farm out my family—Mama to a nursing home, Neal Grace to T. J.'s, and my grandchild to God knows where—just so I can be with *you?* Well, let me clarify a few things. Yes, I wished for a simpler, less complicated life. And for a while I was naive enough to think a relationship with you might give me that. But I've come to my senses. I'll take these complications over your simplicity any day of the week.

"And here's another news flash for you: I don't *need* to be taken care of. Especially not by some testosterone-loaded macho man who can't see past his own agenda. Go find yourself some simpering brainless dimwit whose sole purpose in life is to worship the ground you walk on. Trust me—you can't handle a Quinn woman. And you certainly don't want to be tangling with *three.*"

By the time Abby was finished, all the blood had drained from Charles's face. His eyes were glazed, and his jaw gaped open. Without a word he got up from the lawn chair, staggered to his car, and drove away.

⌣

"Mom?"

Abby heard Neal Grace's voice before she felt the touch on her shoulder.

"Are you OK, Mom?"

"I'm fine. Or will be." Abby rubbed a hand across her face, and her fingers came away from her cheeks smudged with black ash. "I must look awful."

"Yeah, you've been better," Neal agreed. "There's someone here to see you."

"I don't want to see anybody," Abby protested.

"Yes, you do." Neal took a tissue from her pajama pocket and wiped the soot from her mother's face. "Trust me."

She pointed toward the house. Framed in the charred doorway stood a lanky, bearded man, his flannel shirt and jeans covered with grime. He held something in his hands—a towel, she thought, stained black from the scene of the fire.

It was Devin Connor.

"When did he get here?" she asked Neal. "And how—?"

He approached slowly and hunkered down on the ground next to Abby's chair. "I've got some news for you," he said. "The fire chief is a friend of mine, so he told me. The fire was definitely arson. The back door had been broken in, and an accelerant was used—gasoline, they think."

"So Mama didn't have anything to do with it," Abby said, with just a hint of question and relief.

He shook his head. "Why would you think that?"

Abby bit her lip. "I didn't want to. But she has left the stove on a couple of times. I didn't dare say anything. Didn't want people to think she's incompetent."

Devin smiled. "Incompetent? Your mother is one of the most competent people I've ever met," he said with a chuckle. "She's quite a wonderful woman."

"Yes, she is." Abby looked up at Neal.

"The investigators believe the fire started around four-thirty this morning," Devin went on. "Your neighbors at the end of the street were up feeding their baby and saw a motorcycle roar by their house about that time."

"Mike Damatto?"

Neal Grace nodded. "Earlier this morning the police questioned me, and I told them about our argument last night."

"They arrested him a few minutes ago," Devin added. "He confessed. Said he did it to get Neal back." He shrugged. "Incredible, what some people will do."

"I'm sorry, Mom," Neal said in a quiet voice. "I guess this is all my fault."

"No, it's not your fault," Abby corrected. "You made a mistake getting involved with the wrong person, but—" She paused. "If that were a crime, half the population would be behind bars—myself included. You're not responsible for what he did."

Devin cleared his throat. "Once the hot spots were controlled, the chief let me in, and I poked around a little. Hope you don't mind. I'm afraid most everything is ruined. But I did find this—" He held out the dirty towel.

Abby took the lumpy parcel from his hands and unwrapped the towel. She looked up into his soot-streaked face. "I can't believe you found this, Devin. Thank you." Carefully she laid the towel on her lap and took in a quick breath. "The Wishing Jar!"

"Wishing Jar?" he repeated.

"Yes. This has been in our family for nearly a hundred years. My great-grandmother, Gracie Quinn, called it the Wishing Jar and said it had magical properties." She traced her finger over the red and gold of the phoenix. "But only for those who were pure of heart and faithful of soul."

Devin smiled. "Then I suppose all *your* wishes have come true," he said gently.

"Not exactly." Abby turned the jar over in her hands. The white porcelain was crusted and smudged, but other than a small hairline crack running down either side, the jar was intact. "I can't imagine how this survived."

"Magic," a voice behind her said.

Abby turned. "Mama! Are you feeling better?"

"I'm fine. Hello, Devin. Nice to see you again."

Devin took her mother's hand and helped her to one of the folding chairs as if he were ushering a queen to her throne. She leaned over and touched the phoenix jar gently. "Well, at least one bit of Quinn history came through the fire."

Abby nodded. "It's cracked, but still in one piece."

"Cracked?" An inscrutable expression flitted over her mother's face. "Hmm. I wonder—" She sighed and shook her head. "Like our family, I suppose. A few flaws here and there just add character."

Abby stared down at the jar. The sunlight coming over her shoulder flashed across the gilding of the phoenix's feathers, and even amid the grime and dirt, the bird seemed to stir and flutter.

"Are you going to make a wish, Mom?" Neal Grace asked.

"I think I've made enough wishes." Abby reached out and gripped her daughter's hand. "As long as you and your grandmother are with me, what else do I have to wish for? Except maybe an answer to our current housing dilemma."

Devin gazed at her, his bright eyes warming her soul even as the morning sun warmed her back. "If I might be permitted a suggestion—"

"There are three of us," Abby reminded him, "and one on the way. We're likely to be homeless for several months."

"But you will rebuild," Devin said firmly. "Quinn House will live again. And in the meantime, I think I might have a solution for you."

⁓

Abby rode in Devin's truck with the Wishing Jar on her lap. Neal Grace and Mama followed behind in the car. She didn't for a moment think that anything Devin had access to would be workable for them, but she was intensely curious about what he had in mind. And it was an excuse to be near him, even if—

"Abby," he said as they turned off Charlotte Street onto the highway, "there's something I'd like to say to you. I'm not sure it's quite the right time, given everything you've been through, but if I wait too long, I may regret it."

She turned toward him. "Say whatever you want, Devin."

His Adam's apple worked up and down. He cleared his throat, mumbled something she couldn't hear, then tried again. "The first time I met you," he managed at last, "I felt something I hadn't felt in a very long time. Not since I lost my wife and daughter."

"You've never told me about them."

"I know. It's difficult to talk about. But someday—soon—I will tell you. I'll tell you everything."

"I'd like to know everything, Devin," she said quietly.

He turned to look at her, his blue eyes bright with astonishment. "I've spent a lot of years carving out a life for myself," he went on. "A life that has meaning. A life of peace and beauty and music and creativity. And for a very long time I thought it was enough. But something's missing."

"What's missing?" Abby asked.

He bit his lip. "Someone to share it with. But not just someone. You."

Her heart began to hammer in her chest. "Me?"

"Yes." He exhaled heavily. "I didn't plan for this, Abby, but I think I might be falling in love with you."

She clutched the Wishing Jar tighter to still the shaking of her hands. "And you never told me?"

"I didn't want to interfere with your plans, your dreams, your wishes. Your *engagement*."

"I'm no longer engaged," Abby whispered.

"I'm glad to hear it." He blushed a little and gave her a half-smile. "But even so, I wasn't sure that—"

"Devin," she interrupted, "let me respond before I lose my nerve. Since the day we met at Pack Square, I haven't been able to get you out of my mind. Even when I thought I wanted to marry Charles, my heart kept coming back to you—your music, your eyes, your smile, your . . . your soul. I know you don't have much in the way of material possessions, but none of that matters to me. What matters is who you are."

His features softened, and his eyes took on an expression of wonder. "You're saying it's a possibility you might be able to love me, too? A simple fiddler who plays his music on the streets?"

Abby nodded. She longed to throw herself into his arms, to confess to him that she already loved him. To tell him how his music twined around her soul and invaded her dreams, how his smile brought light and color to her world. But she didn't. Instead, she reached out and touched his hand lightly. "Yes," she murmured, "it's a very definite possibility."

He grinned at her, and his eyes glowed with a light as blue and vivid as the Carolina sky on a cloudless autumn morning. "A very definite possibility," he repeated. "Sounds good to me."

At the road that led to his cabin, he turned the truck off Old Charlotte Highway and began the drive up the mountain. But before they reached his turnoff, he veered to the left and kept climbing—the best Abby could figure, they were circling around, up into the woods behind his place. Maybe there was a cabin for rent up here.

They came to the top of the ridge, crested the rise, and stopped. Below them, spread out in subdued waves of blue and gray and purple, the mountains stretched all the way to the horizon. Abby had lived in the Blue Ridge all her life, and she had never seen a vista quite as stunning as this one.

But it wasn't only the panorama that took her breath away. Built into the rock and facing out toward the view sat a house that rose up like an extension of the mountain itself. It was all crafted in stone and glass and natural wood, with enormous beams and a slate walkway leading to double oak doors that must have been nine feet high.

As Neal Grace pulled the car in beside them, Devin got out of the truck. He motioned Abby and the others to follow, and led them through the oak doors into a great room where a massive stone fireplace rose up two stories into a cathedral ceiling. Glass doors on either side of the hearth led to a wide deck that overlooked the mountains.

Neal Grace poked her in the back. "This is awesome, Mom."

"I think you'll be comfortable here," Devin

was saying. "There's a master suite with a private bath on this level." He turned and offered a jesting bow in Mama's direction. "For you, milady."

"Well, thank you, kind sir," she responded with a little curtsy.

"Upstairs"—he pointed to a broad sweeping staircase that led to a loft overlooking the great room—"you'll find suitable accommodations for the mother and the mother-to-be. The kitchen is stocked, the beds are made, and the bathrooms have everything you'll need, I think—shampoo and soap and towels and all that. You'll just have to buy personal items . . . and some clothes."

Abby glanced down at her bedraggled, soot-stained nightgown and robe. Mama didn't look much better, and Neal Grace was still in her flannel pajamas and borrowed tennis shoes. They all looked like refugees, survivors of some terrible war. "I guess we will," she said with a grin.

Devin took the Wishing Jar out of Abby's hands and set it on the mantel. "There," he said. "Now it's officially your home."

"But—," Abby stammered. "Even with the insurance money, we can't afford to rent a place like this. And what about the owner?"

"The owner offers it as a gift." Devin smiled and averted his eyes.

"Wait a minute." Abby stared at him. "What was all that you said about being a caretaker? You led me to believe you owned nothing except your fiddle and the clothes on your back!"

"That's pretty much true," he responded quietly. "No one owns the land, the sky, the stars, the music. No one except God. Everything we're given is on loan to us. What matters is what we do with it. We're all simply caretakers."

Leaving Mama and Neal Grace to explore the house, Devin took Abby's hand and led her out onto the deck, where the mountains fell away before them in layers of sunshine and shadow. He put an arm around her shoulders and let his eyes wander off into the distance.

"I think I need to explain a few things."

Abby raised an eyebrow. "Yes, I believe you do."

"Before you get your hopes up that I'm some kind of eccentric closet millionaire, let me clarify. This house is not mine. Not by any definition of ownership."

"Then who—?"

"It belongs to my brother-in-law, Benjamin, and his wife. One house among many. They also have a lodge in Aspen, a beach house in Cozumel, and a villa—just a small one—on the French Riviera. This one they use as a retreat once or twice a year."

"Must be nice," Abby mused.

"Depends on your perspective. In a way," he went on, "I *am* a caretaker. I look after this house for them. In return, they gave me three acres and the cabin down the mountain."

"You're telling the truth. You're not rich."

"No, Abby, I'm not. I was, once. But it didn't satisfy me."

She turned and stared at him. "Go on. I'm spellbound."

"I married young, in my twenties. Her name was Laura, and I loved her. In many ways, we were very happy—at least early on. But she was ambitious, and I—well, I wasn't nearly enough of a go-getter to suit her." He shrugged. "She was born to money. I was born to music. For a long time—years—I set aside my passion and tried to become what she wanted me to be. A business tycoon, in her brother's real-estate investment firm."

"Doesn't sound like a very good fit," Abby said.

"It wasn't. I was miserable, and yet I kept on, for Laura's sake."

"What happened?"

Devin sighed. "Shortly before our third anniversary, we had a baby—a little girl named Audrey. She was a beautiful child, the light of my life. When I looked into her face, when she hugged me, everything made sense. When I'd play my fiddle for her, she—"

He stopped abruptly and cleared his throat. "The year Audrey turned six, Laura decided to take her to Colorado—to spend her birthday learning to ski. I stayed home because I had an important real-estate deal to close that weekend. On their way to the lodge in Ben's private jet, they ran into a bad snowstorm. The plane went down, and—"

Abby clutched his arm. "Oh, Devin, how awful! I can't imagine!"

He squeezed her hand and swallowed hard. "Anyway, after the funeral, I began to rethink my life. I had known for a long time that Laura's dreams and ambitions weren't my own. I left the firm, sold our big house in Biltmore Forest, and—much to my brother-in-law's dismay—gave most of the money away. I invested enough of my savings to live on, but that and the cabin are about the extent of my property." He smiled. "I spend my time writing music and playing it. A couple of my piano pieces have been published—but of course royalties on sheet music aren't likely to make me a millionaire again."

"Being a millionaire doesn't matter," Abby said softly. "You're living the kind of life that feeds your soul."

He turned and gazed at her, a look of wonder on his face. "Then you do understand."

"Yes, I think I do. It's a matter of calling. Of becoming who you were created to be. Of living the life you were destined to live."

"I never dreamed I'd meet anyone who might be able to share that life with me," he said quietly.

She reached out and took his hand. "In the past few months, Devin, I've wasted a lot of time and energy wishing for my life to be different. Wondering what might have been if John Mac had lived. And all the while, everything that was really important was right in front of me. Love. Faith. Contentment. Mama and Neal Grace—and now that grandchild she's carrying. And you."

"Me?" His eyes opened wide.

"Yes, you. From the moment we met, I knew there was something different about you. Different—and wonderful. It scared me and attracted me all at the same time. I think we have much to give to each other, much to learn from each other. Enough to keep us busy for years to come."

Devin's blue-sky eyes lit up with that incredible smile. "I won't pressure you in any way," he said. "This house is yours for as long as you need it. No strings attached. Whatever might develop between us—" He tilted his head. "Well, we'll just take that one step at a time."

"You don't know what you're letting yourself in for," she warned. "Quinn women have a reputation for being strong-willed. Maybe even bullheaded."

He ducked his head and chuckled. "I'll take my chances—with all three of you."

Abby's thoughts drifted to the Wishing Jar, sitting on the mantel inside. Cracked and smudged with grime, a bit the worse for wear. Yet still the phoenix soared, rising up from the ashes to a new life and a sweeter song.

She sighed and leaned against the deck rail, gazing out over the mountain vista below. She only had one wish remaining, one prayer left to be prayed.

And it had already been answered.

Epilogue

The Wish That Never Was

Quinn House
June 2003

Edith awoke to the sound of a baby crying. In her dreams, too, an infant had been wailing, until she took the child in her arms and breathed on her. Then the tiny girl quieted, nestling into the crook of her elbow, easing back to sleep.

She blinked back the darkness, overcome by a momentary sense of disorientation. And then she smiled.

Her great-granddaughter. Edith Grace Quinn McDougall. One week old today.

In the rebuilding of Quinn House, a second bedroom had been added on the first floor, and for a few days—at least until Neal had healed enough to go up and down the stairs—the new mother and daughter were occupying the room next door.

Neal had been worried that the noise might bother her grandmother. But how could Edith possibly be disturbed, when her great-granddaughter's every cry was one more evidence of the miracle?

She heard footsteps on the stairs and muffled voices from the adjoining room. Apparently Devin and Abby were awake, too, checking on their new grandchild. In a week or so, when Neal was stronger, they would return to their cabin on the mountain and resume what Edith could only describe as their extended honeymoon. Abby had taken a six-month sabbatical. She and Devin had been married almost four months and showed no signs of tiring of each other's company.

But now that Gracie had been born, Edith knew Abby wouldn't stay away from Quinn House for long. Already she was talking about coming in after work to help take care of the baby once Neal started college in September. And Devin wanted to get in on the act, too. He had no intention, he said, of letting the Quinn women have all the fun with his step-granddaughter.

The sound of Devin's laughter drifted through the wall, and Edith pushed back the covers and slid her feet into her slippers. Since everyone else in the house was up, she might as well join them.

She went into the hallway and turned on the light, pausing to gaze at the gallery of Quinn family photos that hung there. Reproductions salvaged from copies Abby had found in a trunk in the basement that had survived the fire. All the faces she knew and loved, with a few new additions.

Abby and Devin's wedding photo was there, as well as a closeup of Neal Grace and her infant daughter. Abby had taken the picture in the hospital, then had it enlarged, framed, and hung before Neal even got home with the baby.

Edith lingered a moment before the photo of her great-granddaughter, then moved down the hall to the picture of herself and Sam on their wedding day. "I wish you could have been here," she whispered, touching a finger to the image of her husband's face. "You'd be so proud of Neal Grace, of the woman she's becoming and the daughter she's produced."

Sam didn't answer—not audibly, anyway. But someone else did.

"Mama?" Abby poked her head out of Neal Grace's bedroom door. "What are you doing up?"

"Same as everybody else, I suppose." Edith smiled. "How's our little girl?"

"Neal, or Gracie?" Abby chuckled. "They're both fine. Come on in."

Edith followed her daughter into the bedroom, where Neal sat rocking in the chair next to the bed with little Gracie in her arms. "Sorry to wake you, Granny Q. I've fed her and changed her, but nothing seems to help. She's just kind of fussy tonight."

"Nonsense." Edith drew closer, looked down at her scowling, bawling great-granddaughter, and laughed. "She's got your lung power; that's for sure."

"Don't tell me I was ever this loud," Neal protested.

"No, you were worse." Edith leaned down and held out her hands. "Here, let me try."

Neal shifted the wailing infant into Edith's arms, and Edith held her and looked into her face. For an instant—just a fraction of a second—the baby looked at her. Really looked. And in that moment Edith saw Neal

Grace and Abby and her own infant self. And beyond herself, her mother, Abigail, and her grandmother, the original Gracie Quinn.

"Get me the Wishing Jar," Edith whispered to Abby.

Abby left the room and returned with the jar. Edith held it up, and little Gracie reached out toward it. "This," Edith murmured, "is your great-great-great-grandmother's Wishing Jar."

The baby quieted a bit, as if listening to every word.

"It holds a certain kind of magic," Edith went on, "but only for those who are pure of heart and faithful of soul."

She heard music behind her and turned. Devin stood in the doorway with his fiddle, playing a lilting melody that wove through the room and entwined with Edith's words. The tune rose and dipped, like the flight of the phoenix itself—now quiet and subdued, now soaring and powerful.

"Listen to the music of the phoenix, little Gracie," she whispered. "The most beautiful song in all creation. When its time comes to die, it goes down singing. But then, miraculously, it emerges from the ashes to new life again." She paused and looked down at her great-granddaughter. "Like this house. Like the Quinn family itself. And when the phoenix rises, its song is sweeter than ever before."

Edith shifted little Gracie in her arms. "Sometimes we get what we wish for," she mused, half to herself. "But once in a while we're blessed with something far greater than we ever dreamed." She held the child and the Wishing Jar close to her breast. Abby and Neal Grace gathered close behind her.

As Devin kept on playing, the light from the bedside lamp caught the gilding on the Wishing Jar. The phoenix seemed to come to life, ruffling its feathers and stretching its wings.

"You are that miracle, my darling Gracie," Edith breathed. "The wish that never was, and yet came true."

Little Gracie yawned and closed her eyes. And as the music and the love swirled around her, she wrapped her tiny, perfect hand around her great-grandmother's gnarled finger, sighed, and drifted off to sleep.